VOYAGE TO VALHALLA

stack
7.2.08

Nearing the wood Paula turned, raising a finger. 'Listen!' Chris and Davy stopped, straining their ears. 'D'you hear it?'

Chris nodded. 'Sounds like a dog. Whining.'

'Sounds as though it's stuck down a hole. Come on!' said Davy.

They worked their way along the bank, peering into every hole large enough to contain a dog, until they came across Gyp, old Sam Pogson's mongrel.

'He must be stuck,' said Davy. 'We'll need to dig him out.

With the aid of a spade and fork fetched from the village, the children were eventually able to dig Gyp out of the hole.

Chris knelt by the excavation. 'Hey!' he exclaimed. 'There's summat else down here.' He thrust his arm into the raw clay and pulled out a smooth, round object. His eager fingers scraped at the lumps of clay that stuck to it. He peeled off the last chunk and recoiled, crying out.

The skull gazed vacantly into the sky.

About the Author

Robert Swindells was born in Bradford, West Yorkshire in 1939. He left school at fifteen, and subsequently worked as a proof reader on local papers, joined the RAF as a clerk, and on leaving the RAF had a number of jobs, including printing and engineering. In 1969 he entered college to train as a teacher. While there he wrote his first novel, *When Darkness Comes* as a thesis, and this was published by Hodder and Stoughton in 1973. He continued writing and teaching, but gradually writing took over, and in 1980 he became a full-time writer.

Voyage to Valhalla

Robert Swindells

Illustrated by Victor G. Ambrus

KNIGHT BOOKS
Hodder Headline PLC

Text copyright © 1976 Robert Swindells
Illustration copyright © 1976 Hodder and Stoughton Ltd
First published in 1976 by Knight Books
Second impression 1985
This edition 1994

10 9 8 7 6 5 4 3 2 1

A catalogue record for this title is available from the
British Library.

ISBN 0 340 59054 8

Typeset by Hewer Text Composition Services, Edinburgh
Printed and bound in Great Britain by
Cox and Wyman Ltd, Reading

Hodder and Stoughton Children's Books
A Division of Hodder Headline PLC
338 Euston Road
London NW1 3BH

For Donald, David, Peter and Elizabeth:
also for our dad and mum.

1

Davy made it to the top of the wall and stopped, one leg over. 'Hey: he's put a dirty great shed or summat where the goosegogs were: they're all gone!'

1

Chris turned up a scornful face. 'Oh aye? I bet there's little green men and all, scrumping! Shove over so I can grip the top.' He hooked his fingers in a crack, scrabbling with his toes. Paula bent, getting a thin shoulder under his bottom, and pushed.

'No; I'm not kidding, Chris. Get yourself up and see.'

Chris grabbed the top and flexed his arms, lifting his weight off Paula. He got one elbow over and swung a foot, rolling up beside his friend. 'Wow! You weren't kidding, man. What's it supposed to be?'

'Dunno. Mebbe a place for his cars: museum, like.'

Paula stood, fists on hips, glaring. 'O.K., O.K.! I wondered what all the whispering was about coming down Fell Lane. You've had your little laugh, except that I'm not *that* soft in the head: now pull me up. We'll get some of his crummy green apples, anyway.' The boys exchanged shrugs and leaned, taking her bony wrists and yanking her easily aloft. She hung with both elbows over, gaping.

In front of them and to either side stretched the orchard, with the big house beyond. But, to their left, covering all the ground where the long, bush-covered mound had been, was the shed. It was enormous: long, low, made of pale clean planking; one end within a few metres of the wall; the other way over where the trees thinned; almost on the driveway. No door was visible.

'See!'

'Typical, flamin' woman!'

'Don't try talking like your old man,' said Paula venomously.

Chris flushed. 'How do you know how my old man talks?'

''Cause you can hear him all over the village, that's how. Anyway, there's still apples.'

'Aye,' said Davy uneasily. 'But the old nut-case might be about somewhere.'

'Is he heck! Who'd hang about all day in a mucky dump like *that*?' She nodded at the house through the tangled orchard. 'He'll be off looking for beat-up old cars or summat. Anyway: we were coming here for apples long before he moved in. Get down, if you're not too scared!'

Chris looked doubtfully towards the house then down into the long grass. He didn't fancy it really, but if he waited any longer *she'd* jump first and then go on about it all day. He jumped, rolled over and stood up. Paula hit the ground in a perfect squash-landing and turned, daring Davy with her eyes so that he launched himself too.

Chris went slowly through the trees to the

3

shed. 'It's all new wood,' he called, unnecessarily. The others joined him, touching the rough planking; sniffing the resin on their fingers.

'I wonder if the goosegogs are still there, inside?' whispered Davy.

'Well, *I'm* not off in to find out!' retorted Chris.

'He'd have to take the mound away before he built it, so the bushes'll have gone,' stated Paula practically. 'Anyway, let's get some apples. We can use them for chucking if they're too sour.'

They moved away from the shed, stooping to pass under the unkempt boughs. Chris stopped at a laden tree. 'Give us a leg up.' He stretched, reaching for the crotch, then twisted his head round, impatient. 'Come *on*, Davy!'

Davy was perfectly still, gazing away through the trees. Paula moved to offer Chris a shoulder but he let go the crotch, pushing her aside. 'What's up, Davy?'

Davy's head turned slowly towards his friend. He pointed. 'There's someone over there, or there was just now.' The pointing finger shook a little.

'Why the heck didn't you *say* summat, then?' Chris was already ducking away between the trees, fending off branches with his arms, making for the wall.

Davy ran after him and Paula called 'There's no one there, is there hummer!' But she followed. Chris was on top, pulling Davy up. Davy rolled and dropped over without stopping and Paula leapt for Chris's hand. She had one leg over when the shout came and she pulled in the other one rapidly.

A man was coming towards them from the house. The trees hampered him; he stopped, shouting from the depths. 'Yes! You might well run. I'll give you run if I catch you in here again!' Davy got up; just his hands and face over, resting his chin on the rough brick. The man spotted him. 'And *don't* think it'll be all right to come back when I've gone in, 'cause it won't: I've got two Alsatians inside and I'm letting 'em out!'

He wasn't coming any closer, so they studied him for a moment then dropped outside the wall and loped unhurriedly away through the strip of woodland. At the edge they stopped, sagging against the trees, blowing a little.

'What a miserable old pig!' said Paula.

'No more goosegogs *or* apples, it looks like,' grumbled Chris. He turned on Davy. 'And *you*'re a right one, and all; standing there looking at him like a wet nelly; why the heck didn't you yell out as soon as you saw him?'

Davy was gazing back towards the wall, biting his lower lip. 'It wasn't *him* I saw,' he said.

2

At midnight the drizzle, which had set in during the evening, cleared and a misty moon showed between rags of cloud that drifted eastward. Its light fell soft upon the roof of Wemock House and the slates gleamed dully, except where turret and balustrade cast dilapidated shadows across them.

The man came out of the shed, perspiring in spite of the chill and stood gazing through the tangle towards the wall. There was earth on his hands and he wiped them absently on the worn seat of his corduroy trousers. After a moment he nodded his head. 'Barbed wire,' he muttered. 'That's the stuff; two or three strands.' He yawned, stretching his arms. 'First thing tomorrow.' He turned, swung the shed-door to, and snapped the padlock, pulling on it to satisfy himself that it had closed. Then he thrust his hands into his pockets and shambled off towards the house, where a single window spilled pale light on the gravel.

They stood silent in the trees, watching. After a while the solitary light went out. An owl skimmed the wet orchard, calling. And they stood watching, older than the trees.

He liked a drop of ale, did old Sam Pogson, but he never did his drinking at the 'Acorn', because that was where the locals went of an evening and he liked to take *his* liquor among friends. It was a four mile bus ride into Tanley, and sixty pence for him and the dog, but they didn't think he was a peculiar old chap in the 'Swan'. They liked to see him, in fact, and sometimes stood him so many pints that he missed the last bus home.

So here he was, walking it back to the village as usual and the dog up in front, a pale blob, working the dripping hedgerows. Just before they reached Wemock House it flushed a rabbit and went off over the field. Sam cursed, part-ing the hawthorns with knotty hands, calling. 'Gyp! Hey Gyp: come back 'ere, ye barmy mutt!' But Gyp went yelping after the old buck, which angled across the field to the wood that crowded the wall of the big house on that side. Sam found a gap and squeezed through. The field was boggy and water seeped through the hole in his boot. He cursed again, stumbling towards the wood. Somewhere in there the dog howled, dismally. Sam shivered, casting an eye at the wall to his left. The top of the house was dimly visible beyond. Sam didn't much care for being near this place in daylight, let alone in the middle of the night. Strange things happened here, or so folks said. Nothing unusual had ever happened to Sam but there was something about the feel of the place that he didn't like. Sixty-odd years ago, when he was a lad, Wemock House had had the only orchard in the county that was free of scrumpers. The kids just didn't go there.

The house itself was empty then: he could remember his father telling him that the man who had it built was a wealthy woolman with a mill at Tanley and a fancy for setting himself up as a country squire. A few months in his new mansion had cured him of that, and he had gone off, never to return. Other tenants had come and gone too, over the years, but none had stayed more than a few months in Wemock House. Nobody knew why, and so they made up stories, as people will.

And now they reckoned the place was taken again, by some strange chap who kept himself to himself; driving into Tanley now and then for food and stuff, and talking to nobody. He was welcome to it, whoever he was.

It was dark here, beneath the oaks, and coming straight in off the silvery field he was blind. He stood a moment, listening. A breeze rustled the tops, throwing off rain which pattered on the spongy ground. A muted whine sounded, somewhere just ahead.

The old badger sett showed as a darker shadow along the leafmould floor. Its exits and entrances were scraped out among thick, arthritic roots. Towards one end was an entrance wider than the rest, where the walls of two or three adjacent holes had collapsed.

Farther in, this burrow split off into several narrow runs and the buck, cut off from his home warren, had taken refuge here. Gyp had followed him and, backing up, his collar had snagged a twist of root, trapping him just inside.

Old Sam stooped to the entrance. 'Gyp: come on out! Here boy, here!' Gyp struggled, bringing down showers of earth on his head but the root held. Sam crouched down, peering in. The dog was a pale blotch. 'Here boy; good lad, Gyp!' A frustrated yelp. The old man frowned, fumbling for matches. He struck one, thrusting his hand into the burrow. The dog's eyes glowed, but Sam couldn't see the trouble.

The match burned down and he dropped it, wincing. Raising his head from the burrow he screwed up his eyes until the luminous ball of the match faded behind the lids. He opened them, and cried out. Someone was standing, quite still beside a trunk, gazing down at him. He straightened, stiffly, and backed away, moaning a little through clenched teeth. Ten paces from the bank he turned, plunging towards the field. He ran without knowing that he ran, over the field: crashing through the wet hedge to stand on the moonlit road, blowing hard. And even here he did not pause for breath but hurried on past the house and towards the sleeping village.

He had seen what he had seen, and now the dog would have to look out for itself. Because the man had been standing between Sam and the moon, and the pale disc had shone through him as clearly as though he were a window.

3

'And you can just sit down and finish that slice of toast *before* you dash off; I'm not having you eating toast in the street, showing me up!'

Davy sank back on to his stool. 'O.K., Mum.'

'"Yes, Mum", or "All right, Mum", *not* "O.K.!"'

'Yes, Mum.'

'If you want to work with your dad some-day, you'll have to learn to speak properly. And where are you going, anyway?'

'Wemock Woods.'

'What have you got on your feet?'

'Trainers.'

'Well; you'd better put your wellingtons on. It was raining last night.'

'Very well, Mater.'

'And there's no need to be cheeky.'

'No, Mum.' Davy sighed, wearily, and rammed the last bite of toast into his cheek.

Paula was standing by the bus shelter wearing her waiting expression. 'Where the heck've *you* been?' she demanded.

'Oh; getting my breakfast and cutting my sandwiches properly and changing into my wellies and all that. You know what my mum's like.'

'Yes. Anyhow, Chris hasn't shown up yet so it's O.K.'

Davy was about to tell her that it was not O.K., but all right when Chris came charging round the corner. 'Phew! I thought you might've gone without me!' His forehead was damp under the pale fringe.

Paula eyed him coolly. 'We were just going to.'

Chris ignored her. 'I told my dad about that man who chased us yesterday. He said, "You want to keep away from there: no one ever went *near* that place when I was a lad."'

'Yes,' said Davy. 'My mum said summat like that and all.'

Paula gazed at them scornfully.

'I don't know why you want to go blabbing everything to your mums anyhow. What if they'd said you couldn't go in Wemock Woods any more?'

'Couldn't stop me!' Chris assumed an arrogant expression.

'Huh! Your *mum* couldn't,' sneered Paula. 'But your old man could stop you all right: I've seen him in a temper!'

'Come on!' urged Davy. 'We're wasting time.'

Paula looked at him. 'Where are we going, anyway?'

'Wemock Woods. I want to see that man again.'

'What for? He'll only chase us off.'

'No,' said Davy. 'Not him. The other one.'

'Other one?' echoed Chris.

Davy nodded, his face suddenly solemn. 'You know: the one I saw just before the other one came out.'

Chris grinned maliciously, giving him a hard push so that he reeled. 'You were seeing things, man. You want to get your specs changed!'

'It was the same man,' said Paula. 'It must have been.'

'No!' Davy's tone was sharp. 'It was another man. He was – different.'

'Hell!' Chris grinned. 'Old Davy's gone off his nut!'

'Come on then,' challenged Davy. 'If he's there again today you can see for yourselves!'

The sun was well up and a thin mist hung over the fields. Webs sparkled in the hedges and the air was chill. They walked along Fell Lane, chattering, until they came to the high wall. Beyond, the turrets of Wemock House were grey with the mist. Passing the gateless, pillared entrance they peered up the unkempt driveway, dark with overarching boughs.

'Who'd want to live there?' whispered Chris.

Nobody answered him. They walked on, their chatter subdued, and where the wall turned they pushed through the hedge and followed the high, damp brickwork up towards the wood.

Nearing the wood Paula turned, raising a finger. 'Listen!' They stopped, straining their ears. 'There! D'you hear it?'

Chris nodded. 'Sounds like a dog. Whining.'

Davy glanced left towards the wall. 'D'you think it's one of those Alsatians he's let loose?'

Paula shook her head. 'It's not coming from there. It's in the woods somewhere.'

'After rabbits, I expect,' whispered Chris.

'I hope it's *not* an Alsatian,' said Davy. 'I don't like Alsatians.'

They slipped on tiptoe into the trees, peering between the wet trunks for a glimpse of the animal. Nothing. Paula raised her hand again. 'Ssh! Let's hear where it is.' After a moment the whining began again.

'See!' cried Chris. 'It's over there, by the sett. Daft thing thinks it's found a rabbit hole! Come on.' He ran towards the sound and the others followed.

In sight of the bank Chris stopped. He could hear a dog, but there was nothing near the sett. The others came up to him. 'There's no dog here,' he breathed.

'Maybe it's a ghost-dog,' said Paula in a spooky voice.

'Shut up!' Davy shivered.

Another whine; drawn out and piteous. Chris took a step to the rear. 'Maybe we'd better go,' he gulped.

Paula gripped his arm. 'Had we heck!' she hissed. 'I was only kidding.'

'Well: where is it then?' demanded Davy. Paula was silent a moment, gazing towards the sett. 'It must be underground,' she said.

Chris's expression cleared. 'Yes! That's it. It's down one of the holes. Come on!' He stepped forward, taking the lead again.

They worked their way along the bank, peering into every hole large enough to contain any breed of dog, and thus they found Gyp, who was of no breed in particular. Chris knelt, peering in.

'It's a white one; I can see that much.'

'Brilliant!' breathed Paula.

'Here boy; come on lad!' Chris slapped his knee.

'I think he'd have come out by himself if it was *that* easy.'

Chris rounded on her. 'O.K., if you're so clever, *you* get him out!'

'He must be stuck,' said Davy. 'We'll need to dig him out.' He began scrabbling at the crumbly earth with his fingers.

'You'll never get to him like that.' Paula turned, scanning the ground near by. 'Find some sticks; branches. We can dig with those.'

They walked about, heads down, kicking up the soggy leafmould. After a moment Davy stooped and straightened, brandishing a twisted limb. 'Here: this is a good one!' He returned to the bank and began hacking with the thick end. Gyp's whining became frenzied. The others found suitable tools and chopped at the hole Davy had started.

A few centimetres down the loose earth gave way to packed, clayey soil bonded with tough roots. Paula straightened up, wiping her flushed face with the back of a hand. 'It's no good,' she gasped. 'My stick's getting split. It's gone soft at the end.' The boys stopped digging. Chris threw down his branch.

'We can't just leave him here.'

'We're not going to.' Paula nodded towards the village. 'You're the best runner, Chris. Go and fetch a spade. We'll stay here so the poor thing won't think we've left it.'

He would have argued if she hadn't put in that bit about his being the best runner. As it was he went at once, swerving away between the trees. With his eye-corner Davy watched Paula's faint smile. Sometimes it seemed that Paula, not Chris, was running this gang.

Chris made good time and returned half an hour later carrying a spade and a fork. The boys got to work under Paula's supervisory eye. It was tough going and took a long time. Davy's fork bared the roots and Chris chopped through them with the spade. Gyp, feeling his rescue near, yelped excitedly, and when they stopped to eat sandwiches he whined piteously, as though begging them not to abandon their efforts.

At length the hole was sufficiently enlarged for them to see what was holding the dog, and Paula, lying full-length, reached in and unhooked the collar from the root. She held on to it while Gyp backed out.

'It's Gyp!' cried Davy. 'Old Sam Pogson's dog.'

'I know,' said Paula, cradling the grateful animal in her arms while Gyp nuzzled her face and neck. 'We'd better take him home now. Old Sam'll be wondering where he's got to: I bet he's been stuck in there all night.'

Chris was kneeling by the excavation. 'Hey!' he yelled. 'There's summat else down here.' He lay on his stomach, thrust his arms into the raw clay and rolled over, holding something in his hands. It was smooth and round and he laid it on the ground. The others came close, peering over his shoulder. His eager fingers scraped at the lumps of clay that stuck to it. He peeled off the last, large chunk and recoiled, crying out. The skull gazed vacantly into the sky.

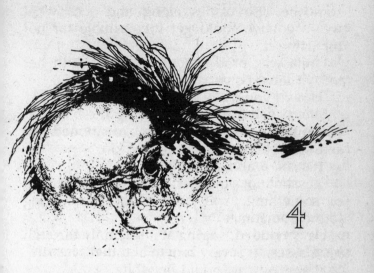

4

They stood in a half-circle, looking down at it. Chris, hands in pockets, touched it with his toe. 'There must have been a murder.'

Davy looked away across the field towards the road. 'We'd better tell the police.'

They looked at Paula. Paula continued to gaze down, frowning.

'Well: we've got to do *something*,' insisted Davy. 'You don't just find a human skull in the woods and not do anything about it.'

'Come on then.' Chris took a step towards the road.

'Wait!' Paula did not look up.

'What for?' Chris's voice was petulant. 'If

19

someone else comes along and sees what we've got we could get into trouble for not reporting it.'

Paula was prodding the banking with her toe. 'It must be very old.'

'How d'you make that out?'

She waved a hand, indicating the bank. 'It was under here, and my dad's mentioned this sett being here when he was a kid.'

'It's *still* a human skull.'

'Yes: but not a murder. It could be a caveman or something. You hear about them being found sometimes.'

Davy nodded, staring at it solemnly through his glasses. 'It *is* very brown and that,' he said. 'If it was new it should be white.'

Chris clucked impatiently. 'What difference does it make? We've still got to report it.'

'Why?' demanded Paula. 'Why do we have to? Nobody knew anything about it before, so why should we tell them now?' She bent, looking into the hole. 'I bet the rest of him's in there.'

Davy's face brightened. 'We could dig and see!'

'Not *me!*' Chris shook his head.

Paula shrugged, turning from him. 'Might as well forget it, then,' she said. 'You're biggest, Chris. We'd never dig it out if you didn't help.'

Chris was silent, staring at the bank. Paula didn't look at him. Davy turned away too, hunching his thin shoulders.

'Well,' said Chris, after a while. 'Maybe I *could* get it out for you. In fact I *know* I could. But when we've got it all out we'll have to report it.'

Paula turned sparkling eyes on him. 'You mean you *will* help us get him out, Chris?'

Chris grinned crookedly, hefting the spade. 'Let's get on with it,' he said gruffly. 'You get into that tree, Davy, and give us a yell if anyone's coming.'

The boy worked for a time with great concentration and much grunting. Paula watched him with just sufficient admiration to ensure his continued efforts.

The sun sank towards the village. Davy climbed down from his perch. Chris heard, and without straightening up turned his head. 'Hey, Davy. Get back up there: someone could still come.'

Davy walked over, shaking his head. 'No. It's late. Anyway, nobody *ever* comes here.' He gazed at the hole, which was now a short trench at right angles to the bank. Chris threw down the spade, stretching. Paula sat on the edge of the trench looking at her blistered palms. A scatter of bones lay at her feet.

'I think we've nearly come to the end of him,' she said.

'It's deep,' said Davy. 'What're we going to do: fill it in again?'

Paula shook her head. 'Not now, anyhow. I'm shattered and we've missed our flaming tea already. We'll put bushes and stuff over it and come back tomorrow.'

Chris took up the skull and squatted in the trench. 'Look: you can see where it goes. This must be one of his arms.' He touched a long bone. 'Then there's some ribs; only about three, though. And a leg-bone there, and part of another that we haven't dug out yet, and a pelvis. Funny.' He frowned thoughtfully. 'It looks face downwards. I always thought they buried people lying on their backs.' He made to rise, remembered something, and said, 'Oh; and it's *not* a caveman like you thought, Paula, 'cause look.' He picked up a dark, shapeless lump, holding it out for her inspection.

She poked at it, gingerly. 'What the hummer's *that*?'

'Iron,' said Chris. 'It was here, just by his skull. Can't tell what it was 'cause it's too rusty, but cavemen didn't have iron things.'

'Mebbe it's the murder weapon!'

'Is it heck!' He dropped the oxidised lump into the clay. 'Summat they buried with him, more likely.' He stood up. 'We'd better get him covered up now.'

Paula looked at him. 'I thought you wanted to report it?'

Chris shrugged. 'We haven't got him all out yet.'

They uprooted scrub-oaks and laid them across the trench, together with fallen branches and handfuls of leafmould. When it was covered they stood off a little to assess their work.

'It wouldn't fool anyone,' said Paula.

'It might look O.K., from farther away,' suggested Chris.

'Yes: about a hundred miles,' said Davy dubiously.

Paula shrugged, turning for home. 'If no one's come near all day it's not likely anyone'll come tonight. Let's just be here as early as we can tomorrow.'

Chris picked up the spade and the fork. 'I'll have to try and sneak these out again, too.'

'Hey!' Davy glanced around. 'The dog: we forgot all about the dog! Where is it?'

'Oh!' said Paula. 'I let him loose when Chris found the skull: he'll be home with old Sam long since.'

They went away; sauntering unhurriedly through the evening wood; looking back from time to time at the sett until it was beyond sight.

The last dusty beams filtered between the trees, casting long shadows which merged, at sunset, into one shadow. The afterglow faded and a scatter of stars hung over the wood. All was quiet. Presently the figure of a man appeared. He cast no shadow, though the moon was high; and the wind that made the grasses nod did not disturb his cloak. He came, silent, to the bank to look upon the grave that he had made.

5

'And don't you come traipsing in again tonight
like you did *last* night, all covered in mud!'
   Davy cast his eyes heavenward and closed

the door. At the end of the path he turned left, as though making for the square, then he doubled back behind the house and headed for old Sam's cottage.

It was early; not yet eight o'clock but old Sam was an early riser and Davy found him smoking in the yard while the dog ate its breakfast. 'By gum! Tha's an early bird this mornin', son. Tha'll cop it, an' all, if thy mother sees thi callin' on me!'

Davy nodded towards Gyp. 'I've come about him, Mr Pogson,' he said. 'Is he all right?'

Sam looked at the dog, then at Davy, a perplexed frown on his face. 'Aye; 'course 'e's all right: why shouldn't 'e be?'

'Well,' said Davy slowly. 'It's just that we found him yesterday stuck in a hole. We dug him out. I just thought he might be poorly or summat, if he was stuck a long time.'

Sam drew on his blackened pipe and exhaled slowly, gazing at Davy through the smoke. 'Oh: so 'e didn't get loose by 'imself then? Well: you've done me a good turn, son. A real good turn. But I'll tell ye summat now as I hope ye'll take to heart.' He moved to the battered wickerwork chair by his door and stiffly lowered himself into it. Then he took the pipe from his mouth and beckoned with the stem.

'Come 'ere, son, and listen.'

Davy stood in front of the old man, who regarded him for a moment with watery eyes, then stabbed the air with his pipestem in the direction of Wemock House.

'Yon place is no fit spot for you an' your pals to be playin' in. I've lived 'ere in Wemock nearly seventy years and believe you me, I know. There's summat there that folks shouldn't go lookin' into, an' I want you to promise me ye'll keep away.'

Davy looked at the ground, shuffling his feet. He wished old Sam had not said that. He liked the old man, even if people *did* call him odd. Sam waited, sucking on his pipe. After a while Davy met his eyes.

'I – I'm sorry, Mr Pogson,' he said quietly. 'I can't promise that. Not now. Paula and Chris and me we've – there's something we've got to do there. In the woods, I mean.'

Old Sam sat sharply forward. 'What sort of "something"?'

Davy flushed. 'It – it's just – something,' he stammered.

Sam sat back, pipe clamped in long, yellow teeth. He was silent for a moment. Then he said, 'Well: I know you kids today are different, what with your spaceships and your television and whatnot. And ye go your own way, an' all, so I'll not try and stop ye doin' whatever it is yer up to in Wemock Woods. But think on.'

He leaned forward again, prodding Davy with the pipe. 'There's things in the world we don't know owt about even now. An' if it's *them* sort of things you're messin' about with; well, be careful, son. That's all: just be careful.'

He waved a bony hand in a gesture of dismissal and Davy turned, going sadly down the path: sadly, because he had had to refuse his promise to the old man. He pulled open the rickety gate, stepping through. Sam called, and he turned. He was still in the chair, leaning a little to fondle Gyp's ear.

'Thanks, son.' There was a smile in the pale eyes. 'Thanks for digging out my pal.'

'It's just like we left it!' Paula ran to the bank, pulling aside wilted scrub-oaks to peer into the trench. 'Nobody's been.'

'Good!' Chris stuck his fork into the ground, impaling last year's leaves, and leaned on it. 'Davy can do some digging today while I keep watch. I've got blisters on my hands.'

'O.K.,' said Davy. Chris strolled towards the lookout tree.

Paula pulled away the last of the camouflage. 'It won't take more than half an hour: we've only his feet to get out.'

She wrenched the fork free. 'I'll go down first and loosen a bit with this, then you can shovel it out.' Davy nodded, watching Chris climb.

He had decided not to tell the others about his talk with Sam. He knew that Paula would nag him all day if he did, even though he hadn't given anything away to the old man; not really. So coming down Fell Lane, when Chris had said, 'I wonder if Gyp got home O.K.?' he had merely shrugged.

'Right: there's a lot of loose stuff now.' Paula clambered out, stiff from yesterday. 'Be careful with that spade; don't chuck any bones out with the soil.'

Davy took her place in the raw yellow trench and began to scoop up the clay. He peered owlishly into every spadeful before tipping it on to the growing pile. Paula squatted on the bank watching him. After a while he straightened up, resting the spade. 'It's all out now. I can't see we've got any further, though.'

'Course we've got further!' Paula stood up, sliding down the bank. 'What *you* mean is that you're fed up already, and me and Chris did it all day yesterday!' She glared at him until he removed himself from the trench, then jumped down.

'Look!' she snarled, turning a flushed face up at him. 'I'm following this leg-bone, getting the stuff loose all round it. You can *see* I'm getting further.'

'O.K.!' He flung himself down on the bank

and waved to Chris, who raised an indolent hand in acknowledgement.

The haze, suspended on breathless air, melted away. The sun beat down on the wood so that its foliage seemed to wilt into limp submission. Thin bright lances pinned tree-shadows to the earth and in their light myriad insects danced.

Motionless on the warm bank Davy gazed away down golden aisles until his vision blurred. When the movement began it impinged upon his vision only as a continuation of the shimmering insect-dance. Until the shifting kaleidoscope of light and shadow fell into a pattern which stirred a memory, and then the man was there, watching from a tangle of trees as he had in the orchard. Without motion, sound or expression, yet projecting an appeal, more urgent now, that the boy should approach him. Davy's eyes focused again and there was change, yet his mind barely registered the change. The trench was gone, and the girl, and the boy in the tree. And when Davy rose, walking with his eyes fixed upon the one who waited, it seemed to him that the very trees were changed: he sensed in the wood some subtle alteration of density, of position, of . . .

He was coming to the place where the trees thinned: where the wood ended and meadowland fell away to the river. But now the great oaks continued so that the wood toppled over the edge and went on down, its dark foliage blotting out the slow, grey water. The boy accepted this, his consciousness sounding no alarm.

Where the slope began the figure stopped, gazing down, and the boy stood a little way off, leaving a space between; following the direction of his eyes.

Figures were moving on the slope. At first he did not see them, for their presence was a shimmer; a distortion, not a blotting-out of objects beyond them; as when one translucent substance dissolves into another. They came slowly through the trees; bent, yet silent in their toil; perhaps because of sorrow. And slowly came their burden, and the object of their grief.

A mastless wooden ship, moving slowly upward as they hauled on its thick, hempen harness; rolling over a raft of pine which crept up the hill as boles were lifted from astern and laid under the prow to pass once more beneath the hull. On the deck, amidships, was a canopied bier and upon this bier lay a man.

The boy's guide turned, slowly. His face was empty and the sleet of a thousand winters was in his hair. Only the eyes lived; eyes that had watched the passage of aeons of hopeless vigil and which now contained a plea; a hope that across the gap which lay between them might pass a thread of understanding. And the boy shook his head, and the words in his own eyes were, 'I do not understand; what do you want of me?' So that the figure moved closer, one intangible hand outstretched to touch the warm hand which reached involuntarily to meet it.

A cry, and the moment was lost. His mind returned upon the echo and he felt the shift; snatching back his hand, falling; falling in the space the shrinking forest left.

'Davy! Davy; what the heck d'you think you're doing?'

His cheek felt cold and there was grass in his mouth. He rolled his head, spluttered, and opened his eyes: a knee, blurred with nearness. He rolled over, clawing a blade from his lips.

'Eh? What you shouting at? What's up?'

Paula looked down at him, her face pale. 'How d'you mean "What's up"?' she said. Her voice was frightened. 'You went wandering off. I yelled about a million times and so did he.' She nodded towards Chris who stood, uncertain, a little way off. 'You took no notice; just trogged off like someone daft. Here: here's your glasses.'

He fumbled them on and the trees unblurred behind her. He sat up and looked round. He was out on the open meadow that sloped gently down from the wood to the river. A memory-shred trailed a fading picture and he said, 'They were down there. It was all trees, right away down to the river. They were pulling it up through the trees towards . . .'

Paula glanced down the slope, frowning, then up, towards the wood. 'Who was? Pulling *what* up the hill? There's no one here. What you on about, Davy?'

'You know!' cried Davy. 'The man in the orchard. It was him, and some others. They had a ship – a dead man on a ship – '

'You're nowhere *near* the orchard!' she said. 'And anyway, if *he* was here we'd have seen him too.'

'Not *him*!' Davy's voice was brittle; his hands trembled and the eyes behind the lenses were too bright. 'The other one. He was watching, like in the orchard. I followed him here but it was all trees and you couldn't see the river and he wanted me to see something and I . . .' His voice faded away and he gazed blankly into her eyes. Slowly the pinched features crumpled and he sank into the grass, rolling a little this way and that as he wept.

Paula, helpless, reached out a hand, resting it upon a heaving shoulder. 'Chris; I think we'd better take him home.' Together they helped him to his feet and supported him, one on either side. Gently they led him away and, weeping still but softly now, he allowed himself to be led.

6

Chris knocked again, more loudly, and they heard slippers in the passage. A bolt clicked back and the door opened.

'Hello, Mrs Bassett,' said Chris brightly. 'We've come for Davy.'

Mrs Bassett shook her head. 'David will not be with you this morning.' She spoke very quietly. 'He had a disturbed night and is sleeping late.' She cast her eyes upward and added, '*If* your knocking hasn't disturbed him.'

'Oh.' Chris glanced up at Davy's window.

'Well; when he *does* get up will you say we've gone to Wemock Woods?'

Mrs Bassett pursed her lips. 'I'm not so sure that I will,' she said. 'He hasn't been himself since you brought him home yesterday. He won't even tell me what happened.' She fixed him with a questioning stare.

Paula slid a hand into his elbow, pulling gently. 'Thanks, Mrs Bassett,' she said quickly. 'I hope Davy'll be O.K. soon: maybe we'll see him later?'

Mrs Bassett waited on the step. Her expression told them to close the gate *quietly*. They did. Mrs Bassett picked up the milk and went in.

'If we'd stayed another ten seconds you'd have told her all about it.'

'I would *not*!' Chris stooped, dragging the tools out of the hedge. 'I was only going to say he fainted or summat.'

Paula kicked a stone. 'Tell 'em nowt!' she snarled. 'As soon as you tell grown-ups anything, they start spoiling everything.'

'Anyway,' Chris changed the subject. 'We left it all open last night. We'd better see if anyone's found it.'

He shouldered the tools as they turned into Fell Lane.

The trench was undisturbed.

Paula said, 'You were in the tree all yesterday. You finish getting him out.'

Chris shrugged, sitting on the dewy rim. 'He's about out, I reckon.' He gazed between his shoes at the bones. 'Just his feet, if we find any.'

'Get the fork. Start just there.' She pointed. Chris began prodding at the clay without enthusiasm and Paula sauntered towards the lookout tree, her hands in the pockets of her jeans. She was halfway there when an exclamation from Chris made her turn. He was crouching: only the pale hair visible.

'What's up?' She hesitated, then began to walk back.

His face appeared over the rim, flushed. 'There's another skull here!' he cried. 'Come and look.'

She squatted on the edge. He lifted the skull, turning it in his hands. 'Wow!' she breathed.

They gazed a moment, then in the silence they became aware of a crunching tread some way off. 'Quick!' hissed Paula. 'Get out of there: help me drag these bushes over—' They scrambled to hide the trench. A voice called and they gasped their relief. 'Davy!'

He emerged from the morning shadows, moving wearily. His cheeks were pale and dark smudges showed under his eyes. He gave them a wan smile. 'I heard you talking

37

to Mum. I wasn't asleep. She wanted to keep me in all day but I sneaked off.'

Paula looked at him gravely. 'Sure you're O.K.?'

He nodded. 'Sure. I think the sun got to me yesterday, that's all.'

'We've got another skull!' exulted Chris. He held it up.

Davy stared at it. 'Aye,' he said, tonelessly. 'You will have. There's another one yet, and all.'

Chris gaped. 'Eh?'

'There's three altogether.'

'How the heck do *you* know, Davy?' Paula's voice was sharp.

'I – I don't know.' A confusion of expressions crossed his face. 'I just *know* there's three.'

'Not going off again, are you?' demanded Chris.

Davy shook his head, looking at the ground. 'No.'

Chris stared at him, then bent to his task with renewed vigour. 'Right! Let's find out if you're right, Davy!'

Paula watched his fresh onslaught for a while. 'You'll never keep it up, Chris,' she told him. 'Let's have shifts.'

Chris swung the fork, dislodging a sticky clod. 'Shifts?'

'Aye: five minutes each. Then it works out

so we do five minutes' work and have ten minutes' rest in between. It'll be quicker.'

He straightened up, holding out the fork to her. 'O.K., I've just done *my* five minutes. You have a go now then, Davy. My blisters are off again.' He flexed his fingers, grimacing, and clambered out.

Paula leaned on the fork and looked at Davy. 'D'you feel like doing any digging today?'

Davy shrugged. 'I'm O.K. I told you: it was just the sun.' He stared at the ground unhappily.

'O.K. then: you're after me.' She lowered herself into the hole. 'Wow! There's loads of new bones down here! And what about *this*?' She stooped, picking something up. 'We could've chucked this away easy! What the heck *is* it, d'you reckon?'

Davy gave the object a single, casual glance. 'Lamp,' he said flatly. She stared at him, and was about to say, 'How do you know?' , when he anticipated her. 'It's a lamp,' he snapped. 'An oil-lamp, and the iron thing yesterday was a mattock, for digging. And don't ask me how I know.' He turned his back on her, walking away. Paula followed him a moment with her eyes. Then she shrugged, placed the earthen object on the rim of the trench, and resumed her task.

The boys sat on the bank. Chris looked at

Davy with his eye-corner. After a while he said, 'Hey, Davy; it's an odd way to bury folk, isn't it; head to toe? They don't put 'em like that in cemeteries, do they?' Davy was silent, gazing at the earth. Chris remembered something and grinned. 'Hey, Davy: there was this Liverpool chap on the telly once and he said they call cemeteries "bone orchards" in Liverpool.' He nudged his friend, who stared at him blankly.

Then Davy began to speak slowly, slurring his words. 'When Mr Procter read us *Treasure Island* before the holidays there was this skeleton.' He paused, frowning as though with an effort of memory. Chris gazed into the troubled eyes, waiting. Presently Davy continued. 'It was pointing to some treasure.'

Chris nodded. 'Aye: Cap'n Flint's Treasure, Jim lad!' His Long John Silver voice raised no flicker in Davy's features.

'Well: what if *these* skeletons are pointing to some treasure? We could find it. We could – set it on fire . . .' He shook his head a little as his voice died.

Chris stared at him. 'We could *what*? Set it on fire, did you say?' Davy remained silent. Chris nudged him. 'What did you say that for, Davy: that bit about fire?'

Davy's eyes were glazed. Chris shrugged,

frowning. 'You're nuts, Davy-boy; I swear you're dead screwy.'

He continued to watch the immobile face for a moment, then forced a smile. 'If *these* skeletons were pointing to some treasure it'd most likely be slap in the middle of old flat-face's orchard with Alsatians all round it!'

'Hey! Are you timing me?' Paula wiped her forehead with the back of a grubby hand. 'It feels like more than any five minutes.'

Chris flicked up the sleeve of his jersey, peering at his watch. 'I forgot.'

'Aye!' Her voice was loaded with sarcasm. 'You won't forget when *you're* digging, though, will you?'

She climbed out and walked over. Her trainers were thick with clay. Davy got up and went to the trench.

Paula squatted beside Chris. 'What were you two on about anyway? I heard summat about treasure!'

Chris told her what Davy had said. 'There's something funny about him, you know: he talks funny; as if he's talking to himself or summat. And he definitely said, "Set fire to it".'

Paula nodded. 'He doesn't *look* right either. Look at him now.'

Davy was standing motionless in the trench, staring at something in the bottom.

'Hey, Davy!' Chris yelled. 'Get on with it: you've had a minute and ten seconds already!' Davy glanced towards them, smiled faintly and wielded the fork.

'I know!' cried Paula. 'Just for a laugh, we'll find out where the skeletons *do* point to!'

'How?'

'Easy! We just start walking.'

'How do we know we're keeping straight?'

Paula was silent, thinking. 'I know: we'll put Davy by the trench. He can bob down and tell you when you're in line with the skeletons. Then you can stop, and I'll go a bit farther, and he can say when I'm in line with *you* and the skeletons.'

'Yes: but after that he won't be able to *see* us if he stays near the trench. What then?'

'Then he can come past you and me, and *you* tell him when he's in line with us. Then you go past him, and I— '

'I get the picture,' said Chris.

They got Davy out of the trench, and he lined Chris up with the skulls. Paula walked a little way into the wood and turned. Davy's head and shoulders were visible over the bank. She moved sideways in response to his hand signals until he yelled, 'Stop! You're O.K. there.' Then he trotted past Chris, coming on. As he passed Paula he grinned. His morose mood seemed to have left him. He walked on, calling back to Chris, 'Tell me when I'm lined up with Paula!'

They continued thus until, on his second walk, Chris came in sight of the wall. He made to climb up.

'Hey!' he called. 'There's all barbed wire on top of the wall!'

'Don't anybody run to look!' cried Paula. 'We've got to keep straight.' Paula stuck a branch in the ground to mark where she was, and ran up. 'Lift me up and I'll have a squint over.' Chris held her by the knees and she placed her hands gingerly between the barbs.

'Anyone there?' asked Chris.

'No. There's a big pile of muck, though, over past the shed.'

'Where does the straight line go?' enquired Davy.

'Bang into the middle of the shed!'

'Well there y'are, then!' crowed Chris. 'It's just like in *Treasure Island*. I bet he's found some gold doubloons or summat and that's why he doesn't want us hanging around!'

'Has he hummer!' scoffed Paula. 'How could he? *We* found the skeletons, not him. How would he know where to look?'

'Maybe he had a map,' suggested Chris. 'With a cross marking the spot.'

'Well, anyway.' Paula dropped to the ground.

'We'll never know, 'cause I'm not off in there again.'

Chris considered a moment, hacking at a tussock with the toe of his shoe. 'Me neither,' he said reluctantly.

'Well, *I* am.' Davy's voice was quietly determined. They looked at him.

'D'you mean it, Davy?' asked Paula, incredulously.

He gazed at her through his lenses. 'Aye. And if you two won't come with me I'll go on my own.'

'Huh! What about the wire – and those Alsatians?' said Chris.

'My blazer will do for the wire – and I don't think he *has* any Alsatians. We'd have heard them. Anyway, I'm off to see what's in that shed.' He began to peel off his blazer.

Paula put a hand on his shoulder, restraining him. 'You can't go in there *now*,' she told him. 'He'll see you. He might be in the shed himself: you can't tell when the door's at the other end.'

'Let go, Paula.' He shrugged off her hand.

'Listen!' she pleaded. 'If you wait till tonight, when it's getting dark, I'll come with you if you really want to look. But not now. Not in broad daylight.'

He looked at her suspiciously. 'You'll come? If I wait till tonight you'll come with me; honest?'

She nodded, reluctant. 'Yes. I think you're barmy, Davy. I mean it; but you can't go in on your own.'

Chris regarded them belligerently. 'Well, don't think *I'm* coming 'cause I'm not!'

'Nobody asked you to!' snapped Paula.

'You must be nuts, the pair of you. Anyway: there's no window in the shed. How're you going to see in?'

'There's bound to be a keyhole or a crack or something,' said Davy. 'We'll find a way.'

'While you sit with your mummy watching telly,' sneered Paula.

'*You* don't really fancy it, Paula,' he told her. 'You *know* you don't.'

She looked at him contemptuously. 'No, I don't. But *I'm* not leaving Davy to go by himself. At least you could come and be lookout man or something.'

'Well, I'm not.'

She turned from him. 'Anyway; it's not even dinner time yet. We've got a lot of digging to do.' They trailed back to the sett with Chris lagging behind, muttering darkly to himself.

Just before tea time Davy turned up the third skull. Since their return from the wall he had worked furiously, refusing to stop when his shift was up; hacking relentlessly at the clay with the heavy fork; stopping briefly now and then while one of the others took out the loose stuff with the spade.

They were sitting on the bank, Chris and Paula, ignoring each other when the hot little figure straightened up.

'Here y'are!' He brandished the fork and the skull was impaled on the tines. 'I *told* you there were three.'

He clambered out, placed his foot on the skull and yanked the fork free. They gazed down at it. There was a large piece missing; a gaping hole in the brownish dome.

'How did you *know*, Davy?' said Chris, baffled.

Davy shrugged. 'Don't ask me. I just knew, that's all.'

'Maybe there's *four*,' suggested Paula.

Davy shook his head emphatically. 'No.'

'Well, I don't see how you can know that for sure,' she said, nettled. 'Anyway; it must be about tea time. What time is it, Chris?'

'Nearly ten past five.' His voice was surly.

'Come with us tonight, Chris,' she cajoled.

'Not likely! I bet *you* can't come either: I bet your mums won't let you out.'

'I'll get out,' said Davy.

'And me.' Paula nodded to the trench. 'Come on: let's get it covered over and get some tea.' They pulled the dead scrub over the hole, uprooting more to cover the new section.

'I'll say I'm off to the Adventurers. They never worry if they think I'm at the church hall.'

Davy nodded. 'Aye: I'll say that and all.'

Chris picked up the tools. 'We won't need them again,' said Davy.

Chris raised his eyebrows. 'Why? Aren't we going to dig the rest of that last one out?'

'No point.'

'We'd better tell the police or someone then. We can't just leave them there.'

Davy turned, a plea in his eyes. 'Oh no, Chris: not *now*. Not till we see what's in the shed.'

'That's nowt to do with it. I'm telling 'em before tea.'

Paula planted herself before him, fists on hips. Her eyes glittered. 'You *do*, Chris Ryecroft, and you can find someone else to go round with!'

Chris stared back at her for a moment, then backed down. 'Tomorrow, then.' His face was flushed but he grinned maliciously as he added, '*If* you're still alive tomorrow!'

7

'Why do you need to take the paraffin lamp to the Adventurers, David?' She watched him from the sink as he opened the kitchen door and a small frown puckered her brow.

'Oh; we're having this sing-song thing.' Davy produced smoothly his prepared story. 'It's supposed to be a camp-fire, see, and they put a lantern on the floor and pile red and yellow tissue paper and stuff round it so it looks like a fire and we all sit round it and

sing. Miss Fellowes is bringing her guitar.'
Miss Fellowes was a teacher at the school.

His mother nodded, though the frown did
not entirely dissolve. 'I see. Sounds more like
a Brownies' sort of thing to me.'

'It's a good laugh.' He injected the right
amount of defensiveness into his tone. 'We
do all these folk songs from all over; some of
'em are dead funny.'

'Quite funny,' she said firmly. 'Or "very
funny"; "dead funny" is a meaningless expression, David: a contradiction in terms.'

He sighed. 'Yes, Mum. Anyway, I'd better
be off. It starts at half-past seven.'

'It'll be a bit light for camp-fire effects at half-
past seven, won't it?'

'We draw the curtains.' He stepped out,
closing the door.

It was a bit light, for camp-fire effects or
for anything else, he told himself sourly as
he loitered along the lane where a tardy sun
seemed to hang motionless over the horizon.
It'd be hours before they could do anything.
Paula probably wouldn't even show up until
dusk. He wondered what she'd do in the
meantime and stopped once or twice to look
back, but she wasn't there.

A blackbird saw him drift into the wood
and dipped away under the boughs, calling
sharply. Midge-clouds, rising and falling in

the yellow light, parted as he passed them, reassembled behind him like a misty veil.

Two rabbits pricked their ears, gazing for a moment in the direction of his approach and slipped underground, so that when he came in sight of the sett he was alone. He slashed with the toe of his shoe at a toadstool, which disintegrated and left a wet smear on the toecap. He had hoped she might be here. The time would've passed more quickly with her to talk to. The hazy events of the previous day worried him, nagging persistently behind his every thought. He could have talked to her about it without her pouncing on his grammar all the time like Mum, or laughing herself silly like Chris. He felt certain that Paula would help him, would at least understand, if only he could talk to her for a while alone.

He went over to the sett, put down the lantern and sat in a patch of sunlight, hacking absently at the crumbly earth with his heel.

Beyond the trees, along the eastern horizon cloud began to form. It moved forward, unrolling its shadow and the golden warmth retreated before it, thickening so that the air became oppressive. Thunder grumbled faintly in the hills.

It began at the topmost rim of his field of vision, and on the dim edge of his consciousness – a smear of dark which spread gradually around the rim then inward, encroaching upon and blotting out the centre until he no longer saw the dry white fungus-juice on his shoe. Without knowing what he did he rose and moved slowly through the trees until the place was right and he turned, blending with the shift, completing it.

He stood once more beneath the oaks and it was night. Silver leaves trembled in a wind he could not feel and their shadows played upon his face. An owl called and he shivered, drawing the cloak more closely about him.

Ve Mork. Darkness, and the grave of his King. Fearful, he peered across the sacred grove towards the long mound, invisible in the night: the mound beneath which Gorm lay, sleeping at last. King Gorm. Gorm of the sagas, resting from battle with his plunder around him, and his glory. Resting in the ship they built for his last long voyage, to Valhalla.

He sighed. Valhalla. An eternity of victorious combats and carousal unrestrained. A fit place for such a man. A place where they would meet again one day, if he bore himself like a warrior and died a Viking's death. And he ached with fear because here he was betraying that high ideal. The sword at his belt had no place on the Ve; nor had the weapons of his friends.

He tried to ignore the words that echoed in

his head but they persisted: the words of an edict learned in early childhood: 'You shall bear no arms in any sacred place, for it is foulest blasphemy.'

They were all here, the others, yet he was afraid. Ve Mork by moonlight is an awful place. In its brooding silence he could feel the presence of the spirits to whom this ground was sacred, and he knew that they ought not to be here, himself and this blasphemous band with its weapons.

Yet he was nearing manhood, and their wish to have him join them in their watch was their acknowledgement that this was so. He smiled a little in the dark, feeling the thick smoothness of his spearshaft. He would make sure they were proud of him. The owl called again and his smile faded: if only he could feel that this was right.

He jolted alert, glancing left. Movement there in the shadow and agitated voices. A figure approached quickly yet noiselessly. Erik, and the sword naked in his hand! 'To the great oak, boy; await the others there.'

He paused, a question on his lips, but the warrior was gone. His heart beat wildly within him. So it was to be now! His people's enemies were out there somewhere in the dark. Scratchers of the soil who watch pigs and run like women from the fight. Yet daring to come here night after night, offending gods not *their* gods, seeking gold that belongs to Gorm for ever, the tribute that will take him to Valhalla.

He went swiftly to where a knot of men whispered beneath the boughs of a great tree. Others joined them one by one and last of all came Erik, his fierce eyes dancing. They pressed round him and he spoke quickly, his voice tinged with savage glee. As they listened to his words the grizzled warriors grinned, nudging one another and glancing in the direction of his gestures. After a moment they began to move off.

Appalled, the boy plucked at Ragnar's sleeve, trotting to keep up with the warrior until he looked down. 'What ails ye, boy?'

'It is forbidden to spill blood on the Ve.'

Ragnar grinned. 'There'll be no blood.'

'But this way is worse; it is no fight.'

'We do not fight with thieves.'

'They are men: they should die as men.'

'They will die like the crawling things they are. Go to your mother if you've not the stomach for it!'

The boy fell back, stung by the insult; then, lest they should think him weak he hurried at their heels.

Erik stopped, one arm raised, then turned, motioning them to come around but quietly. He sank to his knees and turned an ear to the ground. After a moment he raised his head, grinned and pointed downward. 'Here: three of 'em, digging like moles!'

He got to his feet, moving swiftly among the men, placing them where he wanted them. The boy hung back. Erik looked at him sharply, eyebrows raised, and pointed to a place on the ground. The boy took a step backward, shaking his head. 'No!' he hissed. 'Not like this. And not on the Ve.' Erik made a contemptuous sound and turned from him.

Upon his silent order the men leaped simultaneously into the air and came down hard, driving their heels into the earth. They leaped again, and again; their unison becoming ragged: sandals ramming the leafmould.

A cry, and a man scrambled clear as the earth beneath him cracked and sank, falling inward upon itself. The crack lengthened under the pounding feet; widening. The earth shifted, moving inward upon the gaping crack, sinking with a long, rumbling groan until the last man leapt clear and they stood watching the earth crumble into the ragged trench.

And now there was movement: a barely perceptible heaving in the earth. Ghastly sounds rose through the broken soil. And the boy lurched backward, fists clenched to his ears. He shook his head, moaning through his teeth, but the image would not leave him.

He saw in his mind a man heaving against heavy blackness, who cried out in terror till the blackness filled his mouth; who heard the groaning of the earth until it stopped his ears and he heard no more; who fought with lungs of fire for breath and found dead clay; who lay, his senses dying one by one yet living still while cold blackness pressed all about, forming a grave round his living flesh. Before his eyes perhaps a vision of his bones, lying as he now lay, down all the heavy years of eternity.

He sank to his knees. His head was bowed and his hands covered his face. He did not see the first faint flicker that played along the horizon, nor hear the undulating rumble, as of a laden cart upon a distant road.

The men stirred uneasily and the exultation faded in their eyes. A warm wind volleyed sudden through the oaks and was gone, leaving the tops quivering. They glanced at one another covertly, questioning. A summer storm, no more.

Yet they gazed on through twisted oaken boughs and the cold fire that danced there was reflected in their eyes. Piling clouds made mountains in the sky which were silvered with the moon until they swallowed it and became invisible, then rumbled on, wiping out the stars.

The wind struck again; buffeting hotly

between the thick trunks and there were voices in it. And the men looked all around them, unbuckling their weapons, letting them fall. They raised their hands before their eyes and backed from the trench. Weaponless, perhaps they would be driven from the Ve; no worse than that. They whirled, reeling from the site of their blasphemy, as retribution struck. The swelling cloud spat a dazzling lance which whipped earthward, blasting into the ground through an oak which split from crotch to root upon the instant.

As if this were a signal, the roaring sky was torn by a salvo of charges that ripped through tossing foliage, rending boles so that a searing hail of splinters swept the Ve and the fleeing men, reeling from the stunning blast, were cut down in their tracks. They fell writhing to the thunder-shaken ground, shrieking out to the gods who struck them down. And the gods replied with fire so that the blackened bodies twitched and leapt in ghastly, broken dance.

And the voices in the wind decreed a vigil on this place through all eternity: a vigil of blasphemers who must guard their Earth-bound king, till the ship and tribute that lay beneath the ground should burn. And the boy heard, and knew the endlessness of it, for Gorm in his sleep and, more terribly, for his eternal guardians.

And feeling a presence he uncovered his eyes, and screamed. Erik towered above him and in his face a single eye stared madly from a raw and blistered cheek. The apparition, silhouetted by the fires behind, gurgled, pawing ineffectually at its stricken head with charred and handless arms. As the boy watched, frozen, the figure began to topple. As it descended he threw up his arms, shrieking.

Shrieking. He rolled, opening his eyes and it didn't stop. The screaming went on and the dream went on too, because they were still here, whole again; watching him beneath unblasted trees. And now there was Paula, fingers hooked in mouth, screaming. And they were real for she could see them too.

He rose, feeling their eyes on him and went to her; pulled her down so that her face was in his breast and held her, gazing all around.

'I know it now,' he said. 'All of it.' She did not hear and he knew that she did not but he told it, knowing that when it was done they would leave him.

'There was gold in the tomb and the Anglos wanted it,' he said. 'They . . . we stood guard over it, carrying arms on the Ve.' He felt her stiffen and knew dimly that she heard the tongue in which he spoke and recognised a language not her own.

'We stood guard so the Anglos could not approach but they began a tunnel, those three, to reach the gold. We heard the tunnelling and piled blasphemy on blasphemy by killing them here in the sacred grove.' He gazed into the quiet sky, then all around, meeting their eyes. 'What did we *think* would happen?' There was anger in the question. The figures stared, unmoving still, but fading now like images at dusk. 'What could we *expect*?' his cracked voice demanded, and the trees shook their heads a little in the wind. He watched for a moment then shook Paula gently, lifting her face. 'It's all right now, Paula,' he said. 'They're gone.'

8

She had had to set off in the direction of the church hall because her mother was standing on the doorstep. Couldn't wear her trainers, either; not to the club. 'And she'll murder me if I wreck these.' The new leather creaked with every step and the thick heels clacked along the asphalt.

Paula shrugged, turning her eyes to the sky. Cloud-streaks to the west burned orange still where the sun had gone, and the fields lay bathed in an afterglow too soft for daylight, too luminous for dusk; while away to the east cloud was piling blackly, and the land beneath wore a pale and fragile glow.

She frowned. All that way round across the fields, dawdling; avoiding all the boggy bits because of her shoes, and it still wasn't dark enough. She'd be there in about five minutes. She could always walk on a bit, of course; past the house and on towards Tanley. It was going to be wet soon, though, by the look of those clouds. Still: she'd get just as wet waiting for dark in Wemock Woods. Dangerous in there, too, if it turned out to be a thunderstorm. As this thought crossed her mind she caught a pale flickering along the horizon. Automatically, she counted in her head and at 'nine' a faint rumbling reached her. She cast a glance towards the wood and walked on, past the high brick wall and out along the Tanley road; hoping that Davy wasn't in there yet, waiting for her. Thinking of him, she felt a small ache, like the beginning of hunger. Little Davy. Ever since the three of them had started going round together he had been the quiet one of the gang; the passive member that every gang contains, before whom the other members can strut, demonstrating their prowess: the member with whom each might favourably compare himself. A sort of portable audience, unfailingly admiring.

Wherever they went, Davy went along too, but he never took the lead; never initiated any act of foolish bravery or mild lawlessness.

They never do, the little ones with glasses. And now . . .

She stopped, turning; gazed back to where the wood hid the house and its wall from view. She pictured him, sitting on the sett, gazing about through his daft glasses and wondering where she was, and whether she would come. She remembered how he had looked yesterday, lying in the grass; the expression on his face just before he had started crying. That lost, bewildered look. She felt her throat constrict; found herself walking slowly back the way she had come. Maybe he'd tell her about it. Would want to, perhaps, now that Chris wasn't around. Anger welled momentarily within her against Chris. You couldn't talk about anything serious with him around. As far as *he* was concerned everything was either funny or too boring to think about. He was just like his dad; just like all grown-ups, when you came to think about it. They ask you things and then don't listen when you answer them. She saw Davy, trying to tell Mrs Bassett about yesterday, and Mrs Bassett saying, 'Yes, love; but you don't say "nowt": it's "nothing". . .'

She pushed through the hedge and walked slowly towards the wood. With the wall in sight she felt the fear rise within her. Even now, while it was still light, the place was menacing. How would it be, then, to stand inside those walls in the gathering gloom: just Davy and herself with nobody watching out? She shivered, digging her nails into the palms of her hands. Perhaps they could just get a quick look; enough to satisfy Davy before it became quite dark. Perhaps – a stab of hope – perhaps Davy wouldn't turn up at all. Maybe he'd been sent to bed for sneaking off this morning. Then she could just walk away; actually *go* to the club, where there'd be people, and noise, and lovely brilliant lights.

Approaching the sett it seemed to her that her wish might be fulfilled for nothing stirred about the mound. She could leave now; could truthfully claim to have kept the rendezvous and found herself alone. And yet she knew this about Davy: that if he came later and she was not there he would proceed without her in spite of all danger. The old Davy would not have but this strange fierce new Davy would. And she knew this about herself; that she could not abandon him.

She was halfway to the sett when she saw something; an indistinct object that sat atop the sett and which, as she approached, resolved itself into the shape of a paraffin lantern. Something within her turned cold as she ran up the bank.

He lay writhing in the leafmould, his face buried in his hands, and all around, in the trees, staring . . . She heard herself begin to scream; stricken she stood and then he was pulling her down and she buried her face in him and clung tightly. He was speaking but the words were in another tongue and she clung to him for an eternity until he lifted her face and said, 'It's all right now, Paula. They're gone.'

But it was not all right. Because now she knew that she had lost him. To commit herself to him would be to throw in her lot with things beyond her understanding: beyond her desire to understand. She loved him, ached to help and comfort him but there was a point beyond which she would not go. She would stay with him, go with him over the wall to find that which he wanted to find, but her mind would remain outside. Her involvement would be a physical one for the sake of their friendship and where he went to in his mind he must go alone.

The stained face gazed detachedly into her own through the barrier, saying, 'I know it now. All of it.' And her mind said, 'Where are you, Davy? I wish it was all like before.' And she felt the tears hot on her cheeks.

It was dusk. She was calmer now, remembering her promise to herself, and he was cool towards her, sensing it. 'Come on: it's dark enough now.'

'What's that for?' she said, nodding towards the lantern which stood on the ground beside him.

'Couldn't find the torch,' he told her. 'It's all I could get.'

'We're not going in with *that* thing lit up!'

'Why not?'

'Well; for one thing you can't just switch it off if someone's coming, and for another it'll light up everything for miles around. We might as well light a bonfire and have a loudspeaker saying, "Here we come, Mister; it's your shed we're after!"'

'You're exaggerating. Anyway I'm taking it. I'll only light it if I have to.' He lifted the lamp by its wire handle, scrambling to his feet.

'We can't go in yet,' said Paula. 'It's only dusk. Let's wait till it's a bit darker.'

He looked away through the trees, sighed, and set down the lamp. 'All right. It'll not be long now.' Resentment smouldered in him. He had wanted to confide in her but knew now that it was too late. It would not take much to make her withdraw from him altogether and, though he now understood what he had to do, and that by its very nature it was something he would have to do alone, a part of him still needed her to be there.

He pushed his hands into his pockets and mooched about, kicking up the leafmould.

Paula sat down, watching him desolately. She wished that she might make him change his mind, knowing that it was not *his* mind she had been fighting.

Presently she said, 'There's probably nowt in there, you know.'

He stopped, regarding her scornfully through his glasses. 'What's he got a shed for, then?'

Paula shrugged. 'Could be owt: his old cars – or he might be growing mushrooms. One of my uncles grows mushrooms in long sheds.' Thinking: 'It's useless; it's not him I'm arguing with.'

'I bet he doesn't have skeletons pointing to 'em!' He was mocking her.

'The skeletons've probably nowt to do with it. I bet we're just wasting our time. It's disco night at the club,' she added, with the air of the soldier who flings his empty gun in the face of advancing hordes.

'We're off in,' he said. 'You promised.'

'I know I did.' Paula was silent for a moment. Then she said, 'If the skeletons *do* have owt to do with the shed the police'll find out when we tell 'em. Then it'll be in the papers and we'll know without going . . .' Her voice trailed off. At her last words Davy had stopped and gazed at her now so malevolently that she got to her feet and took a pace backwards.

He faced her, his fists tight-clenched. 'No

police,' he hissed. 'And no papers. Nobody must know until . . .' He dropped his gaze, biting his lower lip. She saw in the gesture a fragment of the old Davy.

'Until?' she breathed. 'Until what, Davy?'

For a while he stared at the ground, seeming not to have heard her and, when he lifted his eyes, the mask was back in place.

'Until we have done what must be done.' He turned from her, going towards the lamp.

Paula stared after him. 'You sound like someone on telly,' she said stiffly. 'What're you on about?'

He stooped. The lantern swung in the crook of his fingers as he straightened, turning. His face was calm but the faint smile on his lips was not reflected in his eyes. 'Nowt, Paula. We've just got to get a look inside, that's all. Come on.'

It was twilight now between the trees, and she followed him as he trudged doggedly to the high wall. As they reached it, her fear grew. It was becoming clear that some motive drove Davy: some objective less innocuous than just looking into that shed.

They stood beneath the wall. The weathered brick was dark in the twilight. They listened. No sound came from beyond. Davy put down the lamp and shrugged off his thick old jacket, handing it to Paula. 'Here,' he whispered.

'You're taller. Chuck it over.' She swung it. One ragged sleeve went over and the garment settled on the ragged wire. Davy jerked his head. 'You first.'

Paula climbed, thinking about her new shoes. She hung, scanning the darkening orchard narrowly before pulling herself right up. The shed was a pale oblong. All was quiet. She reached down, hauling Davy up. He winced as a barb penetrated the jacket. 'Ssh!' hissed Paula.

They straddled the wall, listening. A tree creaked a little in the wind and grassheads clashed softly below. A window in the house was faintly luminous, as though with light from a room farther in. They watched it for a while but nothing moved beyond.

Davy gestured down. 'You drop, and I'll pass you the lamp.'

Paula chewed her lip, hesitating. 'You sure you want to do this?' she breathed.

'Yes. Get going.'

She inhaled to check her trembling, and dropped. She crouched in the high grass, watching. Nothing. She straightened. 'Come on.' Davy, half-silhouette now, handed down the lamp. It clinked on the brickwork, and they held their breath and looked towards the house. The tree creaked again and the grass hissed conspiratorially. Davy dropped into the sound. They waited close by the wall. The wind gusted and there was rain in it. Davy laid a restraining hand on Paula's arm. 'Wait.' He smiled a little, looking at the sky. She watched him sidelong. Almost as though . . .

The wind rose from the east, driving before it cloud which smothered the newborn moon. The rainsound swelled until the orchard was roaring softly all around. He leant to her ear. 'Now.' She followed as he ran crouching to the shed. His jacket was on the wall and the shirt stuck to his back like a grey, crinkly skin. They stopped in the piny smell of the wet boards. The rain drummed on the tarpaper roof, falling like a curtain from its overhang. The shed screened them now from the house. Paula breathed out slowly. Davy peered round the shed-end, beckoning with a flick of his free hand and slid away down the long side. Paula followed. The house was a dark blur. If anyone looked out now, it was doubtful whether they would be seen through the rain even against the pale shed.

Davy reached the corner and stuck his head round to see the door-end of the shed for the first time. Paula heard the sharp intake of his breath and when he turned his streaming face to her his eyes gleamed behind beaded lenses.

'It's not shut, Paula; he's left it open!' He made to dart round the corner.

Paula grabbed a fold of sodden shirt, thrusting her mouth at his ear. 'Wait! He might be in there!'

Davy stepped back and peered round again. 'Don't think so,' he said. 'No light.' Paula moved up alongside him to see for herself. The door stood ajar, revealing a strip of the pitch-black interior. A lockless hasp protruded from the jamb. Davy moved forward with the lamp. Paula glanced towards the house, then followed. In the doorway Davy stopped.

'You wait here. Watch the house. I'm off in and light the lamp. Push the door to and lean on it, then no light'll get out.'

He slipped inside, and she backed up to the door, pushing it closed with a faint creak. She blew a raindrop from the end of her nose and stood gazing towards the house. The lighted window was brighter now in the gathering dark. 'Come on, Davy,' she breathed. 'Hurry up.'

It was utterly black. He crouched, pushing out the tray of the matchbox. The match flare blinded him and he groped for the lamp, thrusting the flame on to the wick. It spluttered and he gagged on acrid, invisible smoke. The flame caught and a suffused glow lit the shed. The boy screwed up his eyes, then opened them, crouching over the lamp, gazing out along the length of the shed. His expression betrayed no surprise at what he saw and after a moment he took up the lamp and went rapidly along one wall, moving sideways like a crab to avoid the deep excavation which occupied most of the shed's length. Halfway along he stopped. The yellow light fell on a jumble of objects at his feet, glinting dully on metal. He crouched, running his fingers over them; handling them with silent reverence. Then he stood, swinging the lantern high behind his head. It struck the wall in the angle of the roof and shattered. Oil streamed burning down the wall. Davy sprang away, exultation in his eyes.

'Arise!' he cried. 'Arise to Valhalla!'

Paula whirled at the crash, clawing for the door-edge, and raised her hands to her eyes as it swung open spilling a lurid glow on to the teeming rain, forming a curtain of light. The lantern! She saw for an instant the floor: the great, leaf-shaped depression; flame reflected in a hundred metal surfaces and Davy, bounding along under the wall, his face transformed with joy.

Chris walked slowly down the lane. At each bend he peered along the twilit stretch ahead of him and when they weren't there, made a small contemptuous sound. It was just as he had thought. They hadn't been allowed out.

They were probably sitting in front of the telly scoffing crisps. Still: he had better go as far as the sett, just to make sure. He smiled tightly, kicking a stone into the ditch. He wouldn't tell them tomorrow that he had been to look for them. He'd just say, 'How'd it go last night?' and wait for the excuses. They'd have to admit that he'd been right all along. He grinned to himself, slamming a fist into his palm. 'That's it: I'll leave summat on the sett that'll *prove* I was here tonight. That'll teach 'em to look at me as though I'm scared!' He quickened his pace.

It began to rain as he crossed the field. He hunched his shoulders and ran for the trees. Under the first oaks he stopped, flicking damp hair from his eyes. The trees hissed softly in the dusk and when the wind gusted volleys of droplets pattered on the leafmould. He moved on towards the sett.

They weren't there. He gazed at the dead scrub covering the trench. Passable camouflage now, in the thick gloom. He listened, and heard only wind and rain. The dank oppressiveness of the place closed around him so that he shivered, and was about to turn away when a small sound made him glance in the direction of the wall. A clink, as of metal on metal. He strained his ears, but the sound was not repeated. 'I'm hearing things,' he told himself. Yet he hesitated. Supposing they *had* come after all? He made his decision and moved rapidly towards the wall as the rising wind blew the rain fiercely now in his face. He must be mad!

Nothing. Wait! A pale shape to his left. He ran along and the shape became a garment. A sleeve hung limply, dripping. They were *in* there! He hesitated a moment then began to climb.

The shed showed pale through the rain and the trees were moving against it, so that it was difficult to see whether . . . A crash from inside the shed! He tensed. Light burst abruptly from the far end of the building, glowing on the house wall. In the shifting glow a figure stood silhouetted. Paula! A door opened; a yellow rectangle with a man in it. Coming from the house, shouting. Paula, whirling through light towards darkness, stumbling, and the man was upon her –

Chris launched himself from the wall and ran at the figure which stood over the fallen girl. The man turned as Davy ran from the shed, making for the shadows. He sprang and the boy was kicking in his arms. Chris launched himself at the man's back so that he stumbled forward, crying out, shaking himself to dislodge the boy. Chris hung on savagely. Davy sank his teeth into the arm that held him and the man cried out again, clubbing with one fist until the boy sank to his knees and toppled. Then, cursing, he stumbled back to the shed, turned, and flung himself backwards against a corner. Chris's head slammed into the pine and he fell senseless into the mud. The man stood a moment, teeth bared, gasping harshly, then turned and ran for the shed, tearing off his jacket as he ran.

9

Chris was conscious but he couldn't move his
legs and as they ascended his shoes banged
and scraped from step to step. The jacket was
tight across his chest because the man had
it bunched in the fist he could feel between

74

his shoulder-blades. His head ached and he felt sick.

The man said nothing, breathing heavily as he lugged his captive up into cold, musty darkness. The ascent stopped and Chris's throbbing head was pressed against the boards of a door. A lock scraped, and he felt himself propelled forward. The door slammed as he hit the floor; both sounds reverberated hollowly through the old house.

For a moment he thought he was alone. He lay face down as the footsteps receded on the stair. Then he became aware of a scuffling sound. He jerked erect, his eyes staring into the blackness.

'Who – who's there?' he gasped.

There came an answering gasp. 'Chris?'

'Paula! Yes, it's me. Where are you?'

'Over here, by the wall. I can see you, just.'

'I can't see you.'

'Your eyes'll get used to it in a minute. How the heck did *you* get here?'

'I changed my mind. Where's Davy?'

'He's in here somewhere but he won't speak to me.'

'Why the heck not? Davy!'

They listened. Breathing, not far away.

'Davy! Say summat, you nut!'

'Leave me alone.'

'He's over there.'

'What's up, Davy?'

'Nowt. Nowt you two'd be bothered about.'

Chris's eyes were adjusting to the darkness. He stood up, walking gingerly over to where Paula sat with her back against the wall. He squatted beside her.

'You O.K.?'

'Yes. He hit me in the mouth. It's cut, I think. How the heck're we going to get out of here?'

'He'll let us out, Paula. He's probably just scaring us. What happened in the shed?'

'It was *him*.' Paula's voice was a whisper. 'He set it on fire.'

'Davy?'

'Yes. He smashed a paraffin lamp inside. I think he did it on purpose.'

'What for? What's in there, anyway?'

'I — I don't know. A big hole, and piles of stuff: metal and that. I only saw for a second.'

'I bet he'll get the police on to us for setting his property alight.'

'I hope he *does*: that'd be better than being shut up in here.'

A small sound in the gloom. They held their breath, listening. It came again; a sob, half-stifled. Davy was crying softly in the dark. Chris looked at Paula. She shrugged, and got to her feet. They walked over.

Davy sat huddled in a corner, his head on his knees. There was a large skylight in the sloping roof above his head and a pale light gleamed sadly through the grime. The rain had stopped. They knelt, one each side of him.

'What did you do it for, Davy?' asked Paula, gently.

'I don't know. I had to: I've got to.' His voice was broken; the thin shoulders heaved.

'Who says?' demanded Chris. 'Who says you've got to?' Davy made no reply, but wept softly, rocking himself a little.

'Come on, Davy,' coaxed Paula. 'It'll be all right. He's bound to let us go soon, and we'll say we *all* did it: we'll say it was an accident.'

'It's not that: I'd not be bothered about being in here if I'd done it properly.' His voice was tremulous with crying. 'He came too soon. He'll have put it out.'

'A good job for us if he *has*!' cried Paula indignantly. 'We could go to Borstal for this.'

'Ssh!' Chris laid a finger on his lips, looking towards the door. 'He's coming!'

They huddled under the skylight as the hollow footfalls ascended. A thin wedge of light showed under the door. The lock grated again. The door swung open and they raised their hands, blinking like owls in the torchbeam. The man was invisible beyond the glare. For a moment he said nothing. The beam held them in silent paralysis. Then he took a step inside the room and spoke.

'Well: you were warned, and you chose to ignore my warning.'

Paula was startled. She had expected a rough voice and this one was soft; the voice of an educated man. She wished she could see his face.

'Fortunately for you,' the voice continued, 'I was able to put out your little fire. Nevertheless your interference, and your carelessness with that lamp have upset my calculations.' He advanced another pace, keeping the dazzling shaft on their faces. 'Now I should *like* to release you, but first you must answer a question.' He paused, and when he spoke again his voice was velvet-soft. 'Tell me what it is that you have seen here tonight.'

They gazed blindly into the light and said nothing.

'Well? I'm waiting.'

Paula raised a hand to shield her eyes. 'We – we don't know,' she said. 'It just looked like a hole and some piles of junk.' The voice laughed, coldly.

'Very good. That is exactly what it is: a hole and some piles of junk. Nothing to get excited about, is it? Nothing to – *tell* anybody about when you get home?'

'N – no.' Paula's mind raced. The less they knew, the more likely was it that the man would let them go. 'We aren't going to tell anyone: it's not what we expected.'

'And what, may I ask, did you expect?'

Before she could answer Davy scrambled to his feet, staring defiantly into the light. 'It was exactly what *I* expected,' he said. The tears had dried on his face but the voice was brittle. 'And you've no right to touch it; not *any* of it!'

The man spoke again, and the softness was gone. 'And what do *you* know about it, young man?'

Paula tugged at Davy's trouser-leg desperately. 'Sit down, Davy, and shut up!' she hissed. 'He doesn't know owt,' she said to the man. 'He's a bit soft in the head.'

Davy looked down at Paula and back at his interrogator. He hesitated and in the torchlight the man could see the uncertainty in his eyes.

'No matter,' he said shortly. 'It is obvious now that I cannot release you for the moment.' He began backing towards the door, keeping his face always beyond the light. Paula stood up and moved after him.

'What are you going to do with us?' she cried. 'Our mothers'll be wondering where we are soon.'

The man paused in the doorway. 'I realise that,' he said. His voice was soft again. 'I shall have to bring my departure plans forward, and when I leave you will accompany me.'

He backed through the door and slammed it. The key turned.

Chris screwed up his eyes, holding his aching head. 'What do we do now?' he groaned.

'I – I don't know,' said Paula. Her voice quavered. 'I wish we'd never . . .' She sank to the floor leaving the sentence unfinished.

'It's all your fault, Davy,' cried Chris. 'You drag us along because you want to see inside the shed and then you set it on fire. And it wasn't an accident either: I remember you saying summat about fire when we were talking about treasure.'

'Yes,' added Paula. 'And then you go and make *him* think you know all about it so he won't let us go.' And the voice inside her head said, 'And he *does* know all about it and it's not his fault and you are betraying him.'

Davy stared at them for a moment, blankly, then turned his back and went to stand under the skylight. His uptilted face, faintly luminous, wore an expression of indifference. Anger rose in Paula so that she half-ran to him and seized his arm, jerking him round to face her.

'And you don't even care, do you Davy?' she cried. 'You're so taken up with this thing of your own, whatever it is, that me and Chris can go to hell for all you care, can't we?' She thrust her face close to his. One of his lenses was cracked across and this gave him a pathetic and a rather vulnerable look which reminded her painfully of that other, dependent Davy.

'I can't explain it to you Paula,' he said tremulously. 'You wouldn't believe me.'

Sympathy flickered within her but she crushed it. 'Well you can *try* me, that's what you can do!' she spat. 'And him.' She flung out an arm, indicating Chris. 'We've both had just about enough of your moods and your barmy carryings-on and now we're here because of you. And who were those . . . those *things* that were in the woods, staring? You can flamin' well tell us what it's all about and we'll tell you whether we believe you or not: we've a *right* to know!'

His shrug was barely perceptible in the dark. 'All right, Paula. I'll tell you as best I can.' His voice was unsteady. 'But you'll only think I'm daft and anyway there's a lot of it I'm not sure about myself.' He crossed slowly to the wall and sat, his knees drawn up to his chin. Paula sat beside him and Chris remained standing, leaning on the wall.

'It started that day we nearly got caught,' Davy began. 'You know: when we saw *him*, and I saw someone else, too.'

'But you didn't really,' interrupted Chris. 'See anybody else, I mean.'

Davy shot him a glance. It had begun already,

81

the disbelief. 'I did,' he said coldly. 'That's what I'm trying to tell you.'

'Let him get on, Chris,' said Paula.

Davy was silent for a while, staring into the darkness. Presently he said, 'He was staring at me and not taking any notice of you two; as if you weren't there or something. There was summat funny about him, too, but I didn't know what. Not just then. Afterwards in the woods I remembered what it was but I didn't say owt because I thought I must be going barmy.'

'What was it?' There was an undertone of scepticism in Chris's question.

'Ssh!' He felt Paula's invisible scowl.

'He was standing in front of the house,' continued Davy quietly. 'But I could still see the bit of the house that was behind him.'

Outside, in daylight, Chris would have laughed. Now he swallowed hard, straining his eyes into the dark. The important thing was not to let yourself believe. These things only exist if you believe that they do. His dad said so.

Paula shivered. 'And the skeletons, Davy: how did you know about the skeletons?'

Quietly, Davy told of his second encounter with the stranger: of what he had seen on the wooded slope. 'But the skeletons; I don't know. That's one of the bits I'm not sure about.'

'Tonight,' pressed Paula. 'What about when I found you tonight?'

He nodded faintly, chewing his lip. 'It was a dream, sort of.' In a flat voice he told of the holocaust on the Ve. 'So I know all about the skeletons *now*, but I don't know how I knew before.' He fell silent.

For a while nobody spoke. They remained motionless, each wrapped in his own thoughts and the faint sounds their captor was making far below did not penetrate. The rain started to drum heavily on the roof again.

After a long time Paula said, 'Why you?'

Davy had laid his glasses on the floor beside him and was kneading his eyelids with the heels of his palms. He rolled his head sideways on his knees to look at her. 'I think that boy was me.'

Paula turned this over in her mind. 'You mean you think you were a Viking boy; is that what you're saying?'

'Rubbish,' mumbled Chris, preoccupied with his inner battle against belief.

'Yes. Else how would I know about Ve Mork and the skeletons? And King Gorm's ship; it all fits.'

'I still don't get it,' said Chris. 'Why are you supposed to set fire to the ship, if that's what's in the shed?'

'It's earthbound,' said Davy. 'Because of what they did on the Ve. Fire's the only thing that can carry it to Valhalla.' His voice rose, becoming tinged with excitement, almost with exultation. 'The gods meant the curse to last for ever, because a buried ship could never burn, but now he,' he stabbed a finger at the floor, 'he has uncovered it and I've got to get to it before he gets all the stuff away. Without the plunder, Gorm will lie out there for ever, fire or no fire; it's the proof of his prowess as a Viking and the symbol of his worthiness to enter Valhalla. It must be with him.' Davy's voice slurred.

Chris turned to the wall, pressing his head to the cold plaster. 'I don't believe all this stuff, Davy,' he said. 'We should be finding a way to get out of here, not listening to your barmy talk.' He wished that they were free; somewhere where there was light so that he could slap Davy on the back and tell him he was daft. The trouble was that here in this black attic none of it sounded as impossible as he would have liked it to sound. Don't stand still: if you do you start imagining things. *Do* something. He groped his way to the door and rattled the knob. The lock held solidly. He began slapping the panel with his open hand. 'Let us out!' he cried. 'Come on, Mister: open this door!'

They listened, but there was no response; only the sounds of a distant coming and going. Chris turned towards the skylight.

Davy was standing under it, his arms raised. 'Lift me,' he said. 'I must go, for they are waiting for me.' Chris moved towards him but Paula's voice cut through the gloom.

'No! You're not going out there, Davy. Listen how it's raining; that roof'll be like glass.'

Davy dropped his arms, turning on her. There was a desperation about his movements. 'Look, Paula; I've explained everything to you,' he cried. 'There's just not *time* to stand here arguing. I've got to get out there or it's all been for nothing. Now lift me, for Christ's sake! They won't let me fall.'

'They?' scoffed Chris. 'Who're "They" you keep on about? How come *I* haven't seen 'em?'

Davy whirled to face him. 'D'you *want* to see, Chris?' He waited for no reply but turned back to the skylight, trembling, his fists tight clenched; staring through the rainstreaked glass into the blackness beyond.

The others became aware of a tension in the air. And then he was not alone. Beside him, and close enough for an outstretched hand to touch stood another form, softly luminescent so that every detail was visible to them, while Davy himself remained in shadow.

Slowly, and in silence, the bearded warrior turned, fixing Chris with his stare. The eyes were pale; icy: and yet they conveyed not anger to the boy but a plea; an accusation, perhaps. And Chris shrank from the hurt in them more completely than he would have yielded to their

85

anger. He felt the panels of the door at his back and crouched. Slowly the warrior turned; pivoting soundlessly and Chris saw Paula wilt into the narrowing wedge of space beneath the slope of the roof. A moment more; a shift in the shadow density beneath the skylight and Davy stood alone.

Chris, immobile, continued to stare at the place. He was aware of his mouth and his nostrils; the current of his breathing was cold about them and he felt contaminated, as though the thing had mingled with the air and he was breathing its substance into his body.

Paula moved and he swivelled his eyes to watch her. His paralysis broke and he moved across the room, aware of the cold, flat taste on his tongue.

Davy was standing beneath the skylight. His upturned face reflected a faint radiance and by its light they could see that he was smiling. Slowly he raised his hands towards the square of glass. 'Lift me,' he said softly. 'They are all around us now. They will not let me fall.'

A loud crash sounded somewhere below. Chris and Paula, glancing into each other's faces, started violently as a muffled scream broke in upon the echo. Their eyes went to Davy, and Davy gazed back serenely, his arms raised. 'Lift me, please,' he said.

10

Mrs Bassett lowered her magazine and glanced at the clock. 'It's after nine, Leonard; time David was home.'

Mr Bassett continued to riffle through the file of papers on his knee. 'Club didn't finish till nine, dear,' he said, without looking up. 'Give the lad a chance.'

'He usually comes straight home.'

'Probably having a natter with some of his pals.'

Mrs Bassett stood up, dropped the magazine on to the coffee-table and went across to the

87

window. Mr Bassett watched her lift a corner of the curtain.

'You worry too much about that boy,' he told her. 'He's growing up, and you've got to let him start going his own way a bit.'

The road was deserted and Mrs Bassett sighed, letting the curtain fall. 'I can't help worrying,' she said. 'You hear of such terrible things happening these days.'

Mr Bassett closed his file and leaned forward to slide it on to the table. He stretched and yawned. 'Tell you what,' he said. 'Give him a quarter of an hour. If he's not back by then I'll stroll in the direction of the club and collect him. I could do with a walk.'

'Very well, dear.'

Fifteen minutes passed and Mr Bassett reached for his shoes. His wife looked agitated. 'Put the kettle on, dear,' he said brightly. 'We'll be back in a jiffy.'

She watched him put on his jacket. 'Take your umbrella,' she said. 'It was raining when I looked out.' She went out into the kitchen.

It was almost dark and a bit chilly, but at least the rain had stopped. He moved at a stroll, using the rolled umbrella as a walking stick.

The church hall was in darkness. He walked up the path and tried the door. Locked. He stood for a moment, thinking, then headed for the vicarage, quickening his pace; feeling the first faint stirrings of unease.

The vicar's wife answered the door and called along the passage for her husband. 'But David was not *at* the club this evening,' he said in reply to Mr Bassett's question. 'As a matter of fact, it was a rather thin turnout: a number of our faithful regulars were absent.'

He would have said more but Mr Bassett had turned and was already hurrying away down the path. The vicar watched him turn into the road then went in, shaking his head.

Approaching the hall again Mr Bassett saw someone standing on the path. As he drew nearer he recognised the man. 'Looking for Christopher, Mr Ryecroft?' he asked, anxiously.

'Aye: the missus is worried daft.' He looked up and down the road, an expression of annoyance on his face. 'Big enough to look after himself, that's what I say.'

'Are you sure he *came* to the club this evening?' asked Bassett, and told him what the vicar had said.

They remained a moment in low conversation before moving off in the direction of the vicarage.

Mrs Bassett opened the front door when she heard them on the path. Ryecroft's presence registered as a vague easing of her tension.

'Is Christopher missing too?' Three of them: surely nothing really bad could have happened to three of them?

'Aye.' They brushed past her and she closed the door, following them into the front room.

'Mrs Bell phoned.' She twisted her fingers together and her voice trembled on the edge of panic. 'Paula hasn't come home either. It can't be *too* bad, can it; not with the three of them?' There was a plea in the question. Bassett shook his head without conviction and moved to the phone.

Mrs Bell answered at once. Bassett identified himself, spoke a few sharp sentences, nodded, and hung up. 'She's phoning Chalky, then coming round here,' he told them. 'D'you want to call your wife, Ryecroft?'

'Aye: better, I suppose.' He turned, the receiver in his big fist. 'Chalky's coming here, is he?'

'Yes.'

Ryecroft grimaced and spoke into the instrument. 'Hello: Clara? I'm at the Bassetts. Now look; don't go flying into a panic, but . . .'

Boots rang on the path and Mrs Bassett started for the door. Ryecroft put down the phone as Constable White came into the room. 'She's coming over,' he grunted to nobody in particular.

The policeman raised his eyebrows. 'Who?'

'The wife.'

'Mrs Bell is on her way too,' said Bassett.

Constable White nodded. 'Yes: she said she'd meet me here. Now then, Mr Bassett; perhaps you'd give me a few details while we're waiting?'

The other women arrived together as Bassett and the constable spoke, and the three of them stood in a tense knot, their eyes darting between the clock and the officer on the sofa. Ryecroft smoked with his back to them, gazing out of the window.

Presently Constable White stood up and addressed them. 'Now there's probably nothing to worry about,' he said. 'You know how kids are: watching an owl's nest or looking for badgers or something, I expect. I'll get a car up from Tanley and we'll have a little look round.' He paused at the door. 'If they show up, give us a ring down at the station. I'll be in touch.' He smiled reassuringly and went out.

Ryecroft let the curtain drop and exhaled slowly. They regarded one another through the smoke. Somewhere, a long way off, thunder began.

11

The man paused over the suitcase in an attitude of listening, and a smile flickered in his eyes. Thunder. A storm to keep the inquisitive in their homes. Something was going right for him, then, even now. He resumed his packing calmly, crossing and recrossing the room; laying the things neatly in place. The van stood in front of the house, loaded, and nothing of value remained in the shed. He flicked up his cuff. A quarter to ten. He was doing well. The parents would be worried, perhaps, by now, but he would be well away by the time they ground into action. People are so slow. Most people. Passing the mirror he winked at his reflection. 'But not you, you renegade-archaeologist-millionaire,' he hissed, picturing the heap of precious metal that waited in the van. And as he worked his mind reran for perhaps the thousandth time its familiar rationalisation of his infamy.

What did it mean, when you came right down to it, to be dedicated to archaeology? Years of training: grinding study through countless nights in some dreary student lodging. Thick, mildewed volumes by men long since dead, to be pored over while other young men caroused in the real world with money in their pockets. And after that? When the training was accomplished? He knew the answer to that one, too. Scraping for grants. Going cap-in-hand for financial backing. Begging reluctant governments for permission to excavate their lands. And what lands! Always some bleak inaccessible spot where one was forced to live for weeks on end with disagreeable colleagues, fractious labourers, dust and flies. And for what? Often a quest proved fruitless, and when occasionally something of real value was found it was seized by the government in whose soil it had lain, or else it ended up in some museum to be gawked at by people who understood nothing of its significance. People like the parents of those damned kids.

Well: this time it would be different. This time the search had proved fruitful. Very fruitful indeed. And it was all his. No museum this time. At least no *public* museum. There are those who keep their own museums: private collections amassed unlawfully and at enormous expense, and this time some of their money would find its way into his account. Quite a lot of their money, in fact.

The last drawer was empty. He closed the suitcase, pressing down on the lid as he thumbed home the catches. Get this down, then see about trussing up those kids. They'd wish they hadn't interfered by the time they'd done fifty miles in the back of that van. He'd turn them loose then. Perhaps.

He slid the suitcase into the vehicle on top of the other stuff, leaving room along one side for his captives. He stood on the wet gravel, looking at the sky. More rain coming. No doubt of it. Another twenty minutes and he'd be off with the storm to mask his flight. Lightning flickered on the horizon as he scrunched up to the door.

The rising wind entered with him, buffeting along the passage so that the pale light from the hissing mantles dimmed momentarily. At the far end the kitchen door swung to with a hollow reverberation. He turned, closing the door in the face of the wind and when he turned again a figure stood in the faintly moving twilight beyond the glowing bracket. An instant only; a blink, and it was gone. A trick of the light. He screwed up his eyes to dispel the after-image, grinning wryly. It was as well that he was leaving, perhaps; the place was beginning to get on his nerves. He took the matchbox from his pocket, going towards the stairs.

Halfway up there was a bracket on the wall with a single globe. He turned the stiff little tap, struck a match, and cupped it in his hand until the flame steadied. A faint pop, and the mantle became incandescent. The stairway was flooded with pale light and with the tail of his eye he fancied he saw a movement, as though something was withdrawn rapidly into the darkness above. He stood a moment, gazing at the shadowy landing. Then he shrugged and continued. Gaslight, he mused, produces some strange effects. No wonder the Victorians were inclined to be a bit on the morbid side. Nevertheless, he felt an odd reluctance as he ascended.

When he gained the landing the pale halo below him smeared his shadow enormous on the flaky ceiling. A thin draught which he hadn't noticed before eddied about his ankles, from under the closed doors of empty rooms.

The door of his own room stood open and the light from within spilled on the boards. He approached it with a thankfulness he was loathe to acknowledge. Inside the familiar room he paused to examine his face in the mirror. 'You're really getting jumpy,' he told his image. He felt vaguely angry with himself. A lifetime spent working in the dust of dead civilisations had taught him that the dead leave nothing behind them but the things which they have made. There could be nothing animate in this house apart from himself and the children. 'And speaking of those kids,' he told himself, 'I'd better stop jumping at shadows and get them out of here.' He moved. His image in the mirror slid aside revealing the doorway and a figure that stood beyond. A shrill cry tore from his throat.

He whirled, and the doorway was empty. Cursing to quell his fear he strode across the room and glanced quickly left and right along the landing. Somewhere beyond the foot of the attic flight a door closed. Cold shrouded his skin, seeping inwards, and he had the fleeting thought that this is what it must feel like to be turned to stone. He took hold of himself: whatever happened, he had to carry out his design, had to reach the attic and secure his captives. He had to hurry, too. And somewhere beyond the foot of that stair a door had closed.

There was a bracket on the wall to his left between his own door and the next and he moved with care towards it, yearning for light. He had the matches in his hand and was reaching for the tap, when the door of his own room slammed and the landing was plunged into darkness. He cried out, turning his head instinctively towards the thin glow from the stairwell and as he watched it dimmed, shrinking to a bluish flicker. In the breathless silence he could hear the multiple popping of the starved flame. Then light was extinct save for a thin wedge that showed under his door, illuminating nothing.

He pushed out the tray of his matchbox, felt for a match and slashed it wildly along the box. It flared and he twisted the tap. It would not move. He could feel the flakes of rust under his thumb. The flame licked his finger and he flung the match from him with an oath. He crouched under the dead bracket, breathing hard. The whole house seemed alive with small movements, with things flitting furtively from shadow to shadow. The spiders of fear hung the vault above his head with their web.

He moved slowly, sliding his back along the cold wall towards his room. Reaching the door he flung it open, threw himself into the room and slammed it, resting his back on its panels; letting the light wash over him like balm.

For a time he remained thus, while the pounding of his heart eased, and the cold sweat dried on his forehead. He was being badly delayed and, aware once more of the urgent need to hurry, he went across the room, averting his gaze as he passed the mirror. His hand shook as he raised the curtain.

The window was black. He scowled down, trying to see into the drive; seeing only his own image and a part of the room behind him. He let the curtain fall, moved over to the lamp and turned it down as far as it would dim without going out. That would cut out most of the reflection, and yet: he had looked from this room on many nights with the light full on and still seen . . . He half-ran back to the window, jerking the curtain aside.

Blackness – there, where the village lights ought to be – and the single lights of farms scattered along invisible hillsides – and over there. He turned his head to where the distant lights of Tanley always cast a faint glow in the sky. Nothing. He tore at the window-catch, bats of panic fluttering in his breast. It opened stiffly outwards and at once he reeled back into the room, moaning. Trees. Where the drive should be, trees thrashed in the wind, shaking their dark leaves in his face, swaying with their laughter and the wind's voice in their limbs saying, 'You are alone, alone, alone . . .'

There was no village. This he knew with a cold and paralysing certainty. No Tanley, no barb-topped wall, no drive, no . . . He stumbled across the room, wrenched open the door and ran across the dim landing to the stairs, plunging down; clattering along the tiled passage to fling open the door. A dim figure loomed on the step and he recoiled.

'Good evening, sir,' said the figure. 'I'm a police officer.'

12

'Lift me,' said Davy. 'They will not let me fall.'

The implication of his words was not lost upon the wretched Paula. 'You have betrayed me,' they seemed to say. 'They will not.'

Chris was staring towards the door. 'What the heck was that?' The scream still reverberated on the musty air. Paula shook her head faintly. They looked at Davy.

His smile was cold. 'You saw one of them just now,' he said. 'And now *he*'s seen one.'

Paula moved to Davy, gripping his arm. 'What're you going to do, Davy?'

He shrugged. 'What I have to do.'

'And fetching help: what about fetching help?'

'When I have done what I must do: while they make time for me to do it. Lift me.' He raised his arms.

'Come on; let's lift him,' said Chris. 'He can do it if he says he can. How else are we going to get out of here?'

Paula hesitated: her concern was still for Davy in spite of herself. 'It's high,' she said. 'There's no way down.'

'Come on, Paula,' pressed Chris, uneasily. 'D'you want to see *him* again?' He shivered, seeing again the reproach in the warrior's desolate stare. And secretly, in the dark, Paula shivered too.

'I'll bring help,' said Davy. 'How do you know what *he*'ll do to us?'

Paula stared at the floor. 'O.K.,' she said finally. 'But we'll *all* come.'

'No!' Davy's smile was gone. 'They will help me but not you. You would fall.'

She looked at him in the faint light. 'I – I wish I knew what's up with you, Davy,' she said. 'You're not like you were. I mean, me and Chris always went first before. Now you want to go clambering over roofs in a thunderstorm. I wish I knew what's happening. It's like a dream. It's not real.' She was close to tears.

Chris moved to stand beside Davy. 'Come on,' he said quickly. 'Give us a hand, Paula.' She wiped the back of a hand across her eyes and came reluctantly, biting her lip.

They lifted him until he could reach the skylight. He pushed against the frame, then hammered with the heels of his hands. 'It's stuck,' he gasped. 'I'll have to smash it.' They lowered him to the floor.

'He'll hear,' said Chris. 'He'll come up.'

Davy shook his head. 'He won't come up. They are with him.' He crouched, removing his shoe. 'Lift me again,' he said. 'And turn your faces away.'

The glass broke with a sharp crack, showering them. Davy knocked shards from the frame with his shoe.

'O.K., let me down a minute.' He put on the shoe, crouching among the broken glass. Rain came whirling into the attic. When he stood up he said, 'Right: I'm off now. Don't try to follow me. I'll get help and he won't come up here in the meantime.'

They hoisted him easily and he hauled himself out. They heard him for a moment on the slates above their heads, then he was gone.

The wind cut through the thin shirt and in a moment it was saturated. He scanned the grounds: there was no movement save the tossing of the trees; no sound but the storm.

He smiled thinly and moved down; slithering over the slimy slates to hang like a gargoyle over the low parapet, watching the drive. He froze, hissing a little between bared teeth. Far down the drive, by the great pillars of the gateway a light was moving.

The torch bobbed and swung as the policeman came on, huddled in his cape. His boots scrunched on the gravel. The boy drew back slowly, his face fixed in an expression of fury. He heard the footfalls change as the policeman mounted the steps to the door and, as he braced himself for the crash of the knocker, the door was flung open.

'I'm sorry to disturb you at this time of night,' said the constable. 'But we're conducting – I say; are you all right, sir?'

The man had closed his eyes momentarily, sagging against the doorpost. When he opened them the lights of Tanley still reflected dully off the clouds. 'Y-yes. I'm all right. As a matter of fact I was sleeping when you knocked: still a bit groggy I'm afraid. Now: how can I help you?'

The men's voices sounded quite clearly, even up here, each time there was a lull in the wind. 'Go inside,' grated Davy desperately, the back of his shirt plastered on the wet slates. 'Why don't you go inside where Paula won't hear you?' He jerked his head round as a cry reached him from the broken skylight. 'I knew it!' he snarled, scrabbling his way recklessly back up the wet slates. 'I knew they'd hear.'

Paula's mouth was open for another shout when Davy's face appeared pallid in the frame.

'Ssh!' he hissed. 'You'll have him up here!' He gazed at her appealingly through his cracked lens.

'But we heard someone talking,' she cried. 'There's somebody at the door!'

Davy shook his head. 'No. It's him; he's doing something to the van. Talking to himself.'

Paula frowned. 'You *sure*, Davy?'

'Course I'm sure. Been watching him.'

'Sounded like two people talking,' said Chris.

Davy shook his head again. 'Well it wasn't, so be quiet. I was just finding a way down when you started hollering. D'you want him to catch me?'

Chris shook his head sullenly. 'No.'

Pressing a finger to his lips, Davy turned and slithered down to the parapet, leaning over cautiously. Both men were now visible, standing in the pool of light on the step. They talked a little longer, and once the policeman shone his torch towards the shed. Davy's heart lurched, but nothing happened and presently the man raised a hand and turned away, going off down the drive. The door closed below. Davy watched the policeman to the gateway then crabbed along the parapet until he came to a place where the balustrade was wrapped with tendrils of ivy. Lightning flickered across his intent features as he swung one leg over, feeling for a hold.

13

Old Sam turned up his collar and stepped down
from the bus. The dog hesitated on the plat-
form. 'Come on, ye barmy mutt,' growled Sam,
yanking at the leash. Gyp stepped down gingerly
and followed his master through the puddles.

Halfway up the street Sam stopped short.
'Hey-up then,' he muttered. 'What's up 'ere?' A
police car was parked outside the Bassetts'
house and by the gate a constable stood,
speaking into his radio. As Sam approached
he flicked a button and clipped the transmitter
to his tunic.

'Now then, Dad; what can we do for you?'

Sam nodded at the house. 'What's up?'

'Kids gone missing. Three of them.'

'Young Davy Bassett?'

'Aye: him and two others.'

''Ave ye got a search on?'

'We've looked around. Calling it off now though, till daylight. Can't do much in this.' He looked at the sky. 'Live around here do you, Dad?'

'Aye: top o' the village. Tried Wemock Woods 'ave ye?'

'Aye, we've tried it. Why?'

'Only they were up to summat in there. Young Davy told me. Wouldn't say what, though.'

The constable laid a hand on his arm. 'Will you tell my sergeant that, Dad? He's just inside.'

Sam nodded. 'Aye. I'll tell 'im. Might be nowt, though.'

The constable steered the old man up the path.

'But *why* can't you go on searching through the night?' Mrs Bassett sat on the edge of the sofa, her hands clenched in her lap. The sergeant turned to her, conditioned by experience to expect the brimming eyes; the brave, mobile mouth fighting the urge to break down. Conditioned to expect it, but not to be unmoved by

107

it. He sighed inwardly. Of all jobs, he detested this the most. Missing children. Sometimes he wished that children might be kept on a leash. He began to answer, knowing that the logic would sound to her like callousness. 'At night time, and under these conditions it's most unlikely that a random search such as we're conducting would be successful. A man might pass within five metres of a child and not see him. If we knew *where* to look, even an approximate location, then it would be different. In daylight, on the other hand – '

All eyes swung as the door opened and the constable entered with Sam. The old man pulled the cap from his head and fiddled with it, blinking self-consciously under the eyes of the assembly.

The constable said a few words to the sergeant, who questioned Sam. The parents listened with fresh hope and, when the old man had told all he knew, the sergeant rapped out his instructions and the constable left the room to use his radio.

Sam regarded the sergeant. 'Looked in the old 'ouse, 'ave ye?'

The sergeant nodded. 'One of my men has spoken to the tenant. He's seen nothing.'

Sam regarded him quizzically. 'D'you believe 'im?'

'No reason not to.'

'He's a rum feller, though; hidin' hisself away in that great place. *I* wouldn't take 'is word for owt!'

'He's a vintage car enthusiast, that's all. Built a big shed in the grounds. Wants a place for his collection, and doesn't like company. Ideal place for him.'

'Doesn't like company?' echoed Sam. 'Sounds funny to me, that. Have you searched t'place?'

The sergeant shook his head. 'No. My constable was satisfied, and we couldn't search anyway; not without a warrant.'

Sam nodded, absently. After a moment he said, 'All right if I go now? Dog'll be frettin' outside.'

The sergeant nodded. 'And thanks for your help.'

'We'll come down there if that's all right,' said Bassett. 'Well . . .' began the sergeant, but the three mothers were already on their feet, desperate to be doing something.

'We'll not get in the way,' continued Bassett. 'But at a time like this you can't expect . . .' He waved a hand, indicating the distraught women.

The sergeant nodded. 'I understand, of course. And I can't prevent you from coming down there. But please stay on the road for the moment.'

Ryecroft, at the window, watching the old

man down the path, raised his eyebrows and lowered the curtain. 'Well: there's someone who's not leaving it all to the bobbies,' he mused. ''Cause that's definitely not his way home.'

They stood beside the car and looked out across the field. The distant oaks made a darker stain on the stormy darkness and from time to time lights could be seen moving within it.

Bassett adjusted his wife's muffler and dropped his arm again to encircle her waist, looking through her wind-whipped hair at Ryecroft. 'We ought to be in there looking.' He had to shout above the whine of the wind in the hedge. 'I feel so useless just standing here.'

Ryecroft nodded, holding the cap on his head. 'Aye. If they don't find 'em soon I'm off over.'

In the police car the radio quacked tinnily and the driver stuck his head out of the window. 'Sergeant!' The sergeant was talking with Mrs Bell. He turned.

'Yes, Taylor; what is it?'

'Constable Cowling, Sarge; says he's found three skeletons.'

Mrs Ryecroft uttered a small scream and threw herself into her husband's arms.

'There!' she shrieked. ' I *told* you something horrible'd happened to them!'

Ryecroft fended her off, holding her at arm's

length. 'Don't be so flamin' daft, Clara,' he snapped. 'They've only been gone three hours!'

The sergeant shot his driver a look that made him withdraw his head. 'It's all right, Mrs Ryecroft,' he said. 'Though I fancy it explains what they've been doing in the woods.' 'Which type do I prefer in a situation like this?' he thought. 'An hysteric like Mrs Ryecroft or a cold fish like her husband?' He was striding towards the panda when a dull flash lit the sky and shouting began in the woods.

'It was over there!' cried Bassett. 'By the old house!'

He sprinted down the road, making for the wall; hauling himself up to see over. He turned, hanging by his arms. 'The place is on fire!' he cried.

14

The man stood behind the door, listening to the receding footfalls in the drive. The blood pounded in his ears. He had gained a little time but they would be back, and by then he must be gone. And he knew now that nothing in the world could induce him to attempt again those stairs to the attic. He shuddered. An alternative then. He closed his eyes, trying to collect his thoughts.

Supposing he left the kids where they were? They would be found before they came to any harm and by then he would be far away.

No! He screwed his eyes tight, clenching his fists till the nails dug into the palms. That wouldn't do. They had seen him twice; that day in the orchard and again tonight. And that little one with the glasses was a sight too clever; seemed to know what it was all about. In fact he had been a fool to think it would be enough to take them along and dump them somewhere. They could give descriptions; would recognise him again. And they'd probably seen some of the stuff too, in the shed. They must be silenced. Permanently. He had no choice. But how to do that without going up there again?

He sagged against the door, fists pressed to his eyes. The sickness was returning, and the fear. The wind-driven rain lashed on the transom above his head and the sound was like a voice that hissed at him, drowning thought.

For a long time he remained thus. Presently he roused himself, lowered his hands, and smacked a fist into his palm. Of course! He turned, fumbling at the latch and went out on to the drive. The rain pelted him as he rummaged dementedly in the van and when he straightened he held a jerry can in his hands.

In the act of turning to the house he paused, peering through tossing trees towards the wall. A light moved dimly in the wood beyond and he fancied he could hear a voice. He muttered an oath, turned, and lugged his burden up the steps, breathing hard.

Inside the passage he set down the can and crouched, twisting the cap. The reek of petroleum filled his nostrils. He straightened, carrying the can swiftly along the passage and up the stairs. On the landing he tilted the can and backed up, sloshing the spirit on to the boards; leaving a trail of it as he descended. As he worked, he was aware of a growing malevolence, which hung on the atmosphere, pressing in like a cold fog. His hands shook, but he fought it, knowing that if he fled now, his task unfinished, he was doomed.

Gaining the passage he scattered the last drops over the walls and floor and flung the can aside. Fumbling in his pocket he went quickly to the door, struck the match, turned, and flung it back along the passage.

Old Sam had sent Gyp home. He skirted the woods; policemen don't like people following their own private lines of inquiry, he told himself.

He entered the grounds through the gateway and approached the house warily. He found a clump of rhododendron opposite the door and settled himself to watch; unrolling his plastic mac and draping it around his head and shoulders. There was a light in one of the downstairs rooms and one lighted window upstairs also. A van was parked in the drive.

For a long time nothing happened and Sam had little to occupy his mind except his fear of the place. Remembering what he had seen near by he turned his head constantly, peering through the driven rain and wishing that he was at home with Gyp. Presently he became aware of movement at the lighted upstairs window. He parted the dripping boughs and screwed up his eyes. The movement ceased. He was about to creep out of his hide for a closer look when the door was flung open and a shaft of light pinned him motionless. He watched with drawn breath as the man opened the doors at the rear of the van and pulled out the can. He saw him pause on the step and turn, and he seemed to be staring straight into the rhododendron. Then he spun round and went inside, leaving the door open.

Simultaneously something moved again by that lighted window, and Sam stifled a cry as he saw that the movement was not within the room but on the outside wall. Someone was climbing down the tossing ivy. He moved forward, allowing the mac to be clawed from about him by the branches. Out on the driveway he recognised the climber at once and cried out, mindless of the open door before him, 'Davy!'

Three metres from the ground the boy froze,

clinging like a startled lemur to the dripping creeper. Sam started towards him then spun, staggering, as the passage beyond the door exploded into flame and a figure leaped out and down, racing for the van. For an instant the old man stood bewildered and a voice, a desperate treble that cut through wind and flame cried, 'The others; they're in the attic!' Without knowing what he did, old Sam lowered his head, spread his hands before his face and plunged into the inferno.

. Davy let go and dropped sprawling into the gravel. He was on his feet at once, glancing about him wildly. Lights, down by the gates, and figures on the wall, shouting. The van's engine roared into life and he knew that the gold was lost, that he had failed. His friends were dying and his time was up. The guardians of the Ve were earthbound for ever. Screeching tyres hurled up gravel as he threw himself towards the van. The vehicle lurched forward gaining momentum and the boy followed, shrieking his despair.

Behind the wheel, teeth bared, the man rammed down the accelerator, aimed his projectile at the cluster of torches in the drive, and screamed dementedly as a monstrous figure reared before him; an eyeless, faceless hulk that lunged with a great axe at his windshield. The van swung wildly, cutting a swathe through

116

saplings and when he wrenched over the wheel to regain the drive he saw them; a ghastly phalanx, shoulder to shoulder, a desolation of faces saying, 'This is not your way.' Swerve, and here were more: he perceived that they formed a double row, an avenue, or gauntlet he must run and at the end . . .

The crazed driver saw the looming shed too late and threw up his arms as the plunging vehicle rammed the boards and Gorm's plunder came home. And the roar of their exultation was the last sound he knew. And behind, through the swathe of destruction ran the boy with the fleetness of final hope. The police were in the trees now, all around. He crouched sobbing at the vehicle's rear and a swinging beam glanced off its buckled side, blinding him. He ducked, snarling, groping desperately at his pockets. Shouts. They had seen him and were closing in. He gripped the fuel-cap, twisting savagely, hurling it from him; slashed the match along the hot exhaust and thrust it at the aperture.

Adrift on the ocean of fire and no hand at the helm. Seared, screaming, he ran back along the canted deck as the vessel came broadside on, shipping flame. The great steering-oar swung before him and he clutched with blistered hands and it swept him sideways, dragging his puny frame across the scorched planking. And all about was roaring; roaring of the fire-sea and roaring of the oarsmen, and he fought; dug in raw heels and fought the helm, and slowly the dragon-prow came round into the wind and she rode, great waves of fire passing under her and away aft. And the oarsmen cheered, and he saw laughter in the eyes of his King. And the wind came to cool him, and the rain to heal, and the cloudmaidens sang for his welcome and he set his course towards their voice.

Sam came tottering through the roaring flame and the children were with him, swathed in his garments and holding his hands, one at either side. And men ran forward to pluck them from him as he pitched forward on to the step. And they lifted him clear of falling debris and laid him on the ground as the first engine turned into the drive, its siren screaming.

And when a constable bent over him, to cover him with his cape, old Sam raised himself a little, clutching with raw fingers at his sleeve. 'Get t'others,' he croaked.

The constable gazed blankly into the wild eyes. 'Others?'

The old man rolled his head towards the house. 'Aye. T'place is full of 'em: all ont' stairs an' all.'

The constable looked towards the blazing house. As he watched a section of the roof buckled and fell roaring inwards, hurling sparks that whirled away on the storm. And he felt the grip on his sleeve slacken, and he disengaged the hand and laid it gently beneath the cape.

'And you saw only the one man in the house?'

Paula nodded faintly in the crisp hospital pillow. The man was sitting hunched so that she could see her mother by the foot of the bed.

'All right, love. That'll do for now. Try to sleep.' He got up.

'Wait.'

He paused, looking down.

'Old Sam: is he O.K.?'

'They tell me he's on the mend.' The man hesitated, then said, 'He keeps insisting that he saw men in the house; that they were helping him on the stairs. Must have been the shock, I suppose.'

Paula gazed at him, evenly. Grown-ups always want you to tell them everything and when you do, they don't even listen.

'Yes,' she murmured. 'I suppose it must have been.'

Epilogue

Chris rolled over on to his back, gazing up through the apple-boughs. 'I didn't think we'd ever come here again,' he said.

'No,' replied Paula. 'It's nice, though; the blossom and that. I don't think he'd mind.'

'No. He wouldn't mind.'

They lay for a while thinking about Davy. This mood which now and then descended on them had become an accepted part of their friendship: a wordless mutual sorrow which bound them together and set them apart from others. Presently Paula stirred.

'It's–different here, now.' She was staring up through thin, midge-flecked sunlight. 'D'you know what I mean?'

'Aye. Not creepy like it was. You'd think it'd be worse, wouldn't you?'

She nodded. 'Yes, but it's not. I won't mind coming here now at apple time.'

Chris sat up, hugging his knees; gazing towards the charred depression and the buckled shell of the van.

After a while Paula said, 'Chris; look here.' She was kneeling close to the trunk of a tree. Chris came over, crouching beside her.

'It's just a chrysalis,' he grunted.

'It moved just now.'

They watched, and presently it moved again. A split appeared in the brittle shell. The movements became more frequent, and the split widened until in a flurry of motion it cracked apart and a damp, crumpled creature dragged itself free and clung quivering to the bark.

'I've seen loads of chrysalises,' breathed Chris. 'But I've never seen one hatch out before. I've never really believed they *did*, they look so – dead.' Paula nodded. They watched.

The sun's warmth dried out the crinkly nubs behind the head and they unfolded, becoming papery wings. The creature flexed them until their tips touched, then spread them to catch

121

the sun. 'And to think,' whispered Paula. 'Last year it was just a caterpillar; then that shrivelled-looking thing.' She pointed to the discarded husk. 'And now – ' She broke off, glancing sharply at Chris. 'Hey; what's up with *you*?'

He drew the back of a hand across his eyes.

'Nowt. I was thinking, that's all. I wish Davy's mum could've . . .'

A breath of wind stirred the trees and the butterfly rose in fragile flight.

'Aye.' She laid a hand on his shoulder and they followed it with their eyes until they lost it among the blossom.